"**W**hat's in there, girl?" Weaver's tone, never pleasant, had taken on an icy edge of menace.

"An old woman," Shiva muttered sullenly.

"Dead?"

"Yes."

"Why were you hiding her in the cave?"

Shiva lapsed into silence. What right had this woman to question her? She was not even Shingu.

"Perhaps she murdered her," the flat-faced man suggested. He grinned.

"No!" shouted Shiva, shocked.

"There's blood on her club," the flat-faced man remarked.

Shiva looked down, her fear suddenly grown large again. "That's *jackal* blood!"

"Maybe it is and maybe it isn't," said the flat-faced man.

The body emerged into the light and Weaver stepped forward to inspect it. As she bent forward, Shiva heard the inadvertent gasp of horror.

"Mother Goddess!" Weaver exclaimed. Blood drained from her face.

"What's the matter, Weaver?" the man asked.

"It's the Hag!" Weaver gasped. "This girl has killed the Hag!"

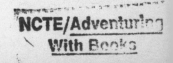

SHIVA
ACCUSED

AN ADVENTURE
OF THE ICE AGE

J. H. BRENNAN

HarperTrophy
A Division of HarperCollinsPublishers

Library of Congress Cataloging-in-Publication Data
Brennan, J. H.
  Shiva accused: an adventure of the Ice Age / by J. H. Brennan.
    p.   cm.
  Summary: As the major ceremony the Star Jamboree approaches,
political rivals from another tribe falsely accuse the Shingu girl Shiva
of murdering the Hag. Sequel to "Shiva."
  ISBN 0-06-020741-8. — ISBN 0-06-020742-6 (lib. bdg.)
  ISBN 0-06-440431-5 (pbk.)
  [1. Man, Prehistoric—Fiction.   2. Cave dwellers—Fiction.]
I. Title.
PZ7.B75155Shd   1991   90-25888
[Fic]—dc20   CIP
                                                     AC

First Harper Trophy edition, 1993.

This one for Orna.

Contents

SHIVA
ACCUSED

1
Death at the Water Hole

There was a body floating in the water.

Slender, outstretched arms had attracted a halo of thin ice, for ice still collected on the surface of the water hole overnight. The feet were pointed so that pale, callused flesh stared up at an overcast sky. The body itself faced down, gently bobbing on small ripples stirred by a chill wind from the morning sun.

Shiva watched from her vantage point upon the overhanging rock, her wolfskin drawn about her against the cold. She remained very silent and still.

There were two tawny cats on the far bank, one drinking unhurriedly, the other relaxed but alert, glancing about in no particular direction. Shiva took them for sisters from a hunting pride or, just possibly, mother and daughter. They knew there was meat close by—the body floated only yards away—but she doubted they would try to retrieve it. Almost all the great cats hated water, and most lionesses preferred a fresh kill to carrion. Besides, they preferred horse or deer meat to human.

All the same, Shiva was glad of the wind in her face, carrying her scent away from the predators. There were some in the tribe who believed no cat would harm her since she had found the Skull of Saber, the great cat banished from the dreamtime. But Shiva herself had no such belief. She lay on top of the high rock, holding very still, waiting.

Although it was almost midsummer, only days from the solstice, the rock pools and water holes often froze overnight; not solid, but with a skin of ice that was sometimes difficult to break if you arrived too early. Even so, the cats and other game preferred the water hole to the river, which was swollen by rain and dangerous. Where it did not overflow its banks, it ate into them, gouging overhangs that looked safe enough until something walked on them. Then they would crumble, plunging the creature into the muddy torrent beneath. Only stupid animals failed to sense such dangers, so most avoided the river, as did Shiva and other members of the tribe.

Most members of the tribe avoided the water

holes as well except when hunting. There was, after all, an abundance to drink in every dripping hollow. But on this morning, wishing to wash her body, Shiva had left the village camp, walked north a little way beneath the towering cliff, then headed westward. Children washed in the camp—when they washed at all—and only a few moons ago Shiva would have done the same, shrugging off her furs and skins without a moment's thought. But of late she found she preferred privacy when her wiry body was naked, hence her visits to the water hole.

Idly, she wondered what she would do if the wind changed, if the cats scented her and attacked. She carried a bone club pushed into her belt and knew how to use it. On the way, she had been forced to warn a young jackal that had grown too inquisitive: There were traces of its blood on the head of the club and she could still hear its surprised yelp as it ran off. She also had a flint blade strapped to her leg, but this and her club would be as useful to her as a frond of grass against two grown lionesses.

Although she carried weapons, her real protections were her flaring nostrils, alert ears and darting eyes. It was unlikely anything would surprise her here. The rock on which she lay was bare, so that

5

she could see anything, however small, that approached close. Even below, by the water hole itself, the surrounding terrain scarcely lent itself to ambush, as there was a lack of any real area of cover. Farther on it was different. There lay the great plains with their reindeer herds and auroch cattle. Where there was game, there were predators, substantial dangers.

Beyond, in a different direction, was the most feared area of all, shunned by the members of the tribe—and by all the tribes who ventured into this part of the world to hunt. There, if you were brave enough to approach, was the sweep of great, dark forest with its wolf packs and its moaning spirits—and her secret friends.

Wary of the cats, she approached the water hole to climb on the rock that overlooked the pool. She stared down and saw the cats; and with them, floating in the water hole, the body.

It seemed to be the body of a little man, short of stature with thin, elongated muscles. He was naked; nor was there sign of furs or skins nearby around the bank. Ritual scarring zig-zagged his upper back on a level with the shoulder blades, a little like the lodge marks of a warrior. Although she could not see his face, she knew he was not of her tribe, for the Shingu used dyes to mark its men, not scarring. Besides, she knew no warrior or hunter of his scrawny build.

Clearly he was dead, or if not dead then so close that it scarcely mattered. Besides, there was nothing she could do. Dead or alive, she would not venture closer to the water hole while the cats remained, not for a stranger.

Shiva waited. She wondered how the man had died. None of the immediate possibilities seemed very likely. Had he come to wash, as she had, or to drink and then drowned? But how had he drowned? The water hole was not particularly deep, not deep at all near the edges where he would have washed or drunk. Even if he had stumbled and fallen, he could have clambered out without much trouble.

Had he been seized by some powerful animal, savaged and killed? The lionesses would not have dragged him into the water. Nor did anything large enough to kill a man live in the water hole. From the distance, she could see no gross marks on the body, no trailing intestines, no meat torn from buttocks or thighs where anything had fed on him. Besides, what predator removed a man's clothing?

Spirits.

As the new thought occurred, Shiva shivered. The world was full of spirits—ancestral ghosts, visitations from the dreamtime, unnatural monsters temporarily made flesh. Had he been taken by the nightwing?

Unbidden, the face of the Crone appeared before her inner eye. Shiva thrust it savagely aside. The Crone had always frightened her, as the Crone frightened so many of the tribe, but recently more so than ever before. In the camp, for moons now as she went about her tasks, Shiva had felt the ancient witch was watching her and did not know why. She had no wish to think about the Crone. She forced her mind back to the body in the water.

Where was his tribe? There were many tribes close by now, in preparation for the great Star Jamboree. To which of them had he belonged? Where was it camped? How far had he traveled to reach this water hole? Had he been missed?

How had he died?

She stopped the questions and did something few of her tribe could do: she watched a picture in her mind. She had always felt different from her tribe. The pictures in her mind were an ogre trait, like the use of her left hand. All of her secret friends could do it, did do it all the time—Doban and Thag and Hana and Dan and Heft the Hunter— but among her tribe, among humankind, the ability was rare. She was certain Hiram had it and

8

possibly one small girl-child called Dawn. And the Crone.

The picture that formed in her mind was frightening, more frightening somehow than her earlier thoughts about the lioness's attack. It was a picture of darkness fitfully illuminated by an intermittent moon, of a slim, small figure moving through an area of rocky flatlands, made alien by night. She could not see the face, but the build made her certain it was the same person who now floated on the water.

Shiva watched this figure in her mind, moving with a brisk, sure-footed gait that suggested an unusual familiarity with darkness. There was no fear in him, not of darkness, not of predators, not even of spirits, which were the greatest dangers of the night.

Yet there should have been fear, for suddenly, in her mind's eye, Shiva saw the wooden club smash down, crushing the forehead and part of the nose so that the features suddenly became a bloody pulp. She heard a short grunt, no more than that, no scream, no groan, for death came quickly.

Shiva shook her head. The picture in her mind was nonsense. Whatever the tribe, no warrior walked abroad at night. Not even men were so foolish as to take so great a risk of offending spirits and attracting the nightwing. Besides, the body floated in the water hole, drowned, not clubbed. It was still difficult to imagine how he might have drowned, but that was no excuse for wild imaginings.

Not that any of it mattered. His death was no affair of hers. He was not of her tribe.

One of the great cats moved away with feline grace. The other lingered for a moment, then followed. Shiva waited with the empty patience of her people, almost unthinking now, although her senses remained very much alert. Patience was inbred, an instinctive response: Those who lacked it died young.

The feline scent faded and died. Still Shiva waited on her overhanging rock. When the subtler sense of danger disappeared, she stood up and climbed down.

She paused for a moment when she reached the water's edge, temporarily seized once more by the notion of a monster of the deep. But experience and common sense told her there was no monster: Had she not bathed here before?

She waded in, and the level of the water was no higher than her waist when she caught the ankle of the floating warrior. He seemed older now than she had first imagined, far older than any warrior of her own tribe. Up close, the smell of death oozed from him like a cloud and she could see the body was misshapen, the spine twisted by age or the diseases of age, the fingers of the left hand clawlike from arthritis. But she drew it toward the bank anyway, holding her breath so that she would not accidentally suck the ancient spirit into her own body. The corpse floated easily, and even when she reached the bank she had little difficulty pulling it out, because it was so small and slight.

She hesitated then, prey to a sudden dread she could not understand. Death was no stranger to her, no stranger to any of the tribe. But this death disturbed her, even though the man was not of her tribe, not Shingu, thus none of her concern.

And yet she felt the dread.

Shiva glanced around, then turned him over. At once a chill hand seized her heart. He was not a man at all, but an old, old woman, wrinkled beyond belief. Her forehead and a portion of her nose had been crushed, as if by a blow from a club.

2
Visit of the Elders

The tribes were gathering.

Shiva's people, the Shingu, had come from the southwest; the Hengenu, the Menerrum, the powerful Barradik, the tiny dark-eyed Henka, all from somewhere east. Then there were the Lees from the north, alone among the tribes in that their council was composed of men; the western Rak, the Tomara, the Karunbara, the Shama, the Labo, the tall Thorangando and more, gathering from their territories throughout the vast, cold land.

Each tribe followed the seasonal shifts of game. Each used the routes and campsites hallowed by its own tradition. All went north in summer as the frost and snow reluctantly retreated. All went south in winter as Mamar, God of Ice, extended his chill grip. But there was little communication between the tribes, except at the great Star Jamboree.

There was a time in every year when the sun moved to the highest point in the sky and the day was longer than any other day. This was the solstice day of midsummer. The Crones could tell precisely when the day arrived, by instinct or by magic—no one knew except they themselves. On that day each tribe held a festival of worship, calling on its ancestors, its totem beasts and its tribal gods for aid in the dark days ahead when Mamar would again pursue them.

But one year in ten, for reasons lost even to the memories of the storytellers, all tribes gathered for the greatest festival of all, the Star Jamboree, when the ceremonies set patterns of good fortune for the decade to come.

At the Star Jamboree, held on a solstice day, the Crone of every tribe made her strongest magic. And the warrior lodges of every tribe danced the ancient dances. And the women of every tribe sang the songs that tribe had learned long, long ago in the dreamtime.

There was much interchange of information— herbal lore, weapons lore, hunting lore, dark witchcraft passed between the Crones. And the women of the councils met together in an extended conclave to agree on matters of political importance.

All that happened at the Star Jamboree itself, but before the great meeting on the plains, there were smaller, more informal meetings between representatives of the tribes. For an event like the great Star Jamboree, there was much preparation to be done. Not all of it was welcome.

Renka, the Shingu chieftain, sighed, not caring that the sound reached the three women ranged before her. They were Barradik elders, their faces dyed purple (since they came to represent their tribe), each attended by a small retinue of warrior men with yellow-painted faces and those ridiculous black feathers in their hair.

Because of the presence of the men, the conference could not be held in the warmth and comfort of the longhouse, for no man might listen to women's deliberations inside that privileged place. Thus the talks had begun outside, in the ceremonial square, but had been stopped almost at once by a downpour of hail, so that they were forced to enter a cavern in the limestone cliff. Like many of her tribe, Chief Renka felt uneasy within caves.

They squatted easily, these visiting Barradik

elders. Their chief, Greffa, fat beneath her wolf furs and attended (Renka noted with faint distaste) by the most handsome of men; Hai-line, a hard, tough bargainer who was also leader of the Barradik hunt; and Saft, the oldest of the three, her face hideously puckered with scarring where she had been gored through the cheeks, years before, by an auroch bull. They said the Mother favored Saft especially, for she had been alone and unarmed and had survived the bull. This was the real reason she sat on the Barradik council, for she was in many ways a foolish woman.

There they squatted, close by the flickering fire, which threw dancing shadows around the cave, politely, firmly, voicing their opinions and demands. Three hard-eyed women, each with three strong men, a dozen Barradik in all. And before them only Renka.

But beyond Renka, half hidden in the shadows of the cave, crouched the still figure of the Shingu Crone, black eyes glittering. She played no part in the discussions, but to Renka her mere presence was enough to bring about a balance. The Barradik elders may well have agreed, for she noticed Saft and Hai-line kept casting nervous glances in the Crone's direction.

"It is a matter," Greffa was saying smoothly, "of custom. We all understand the importance of custom."

Renka nodded. "Custom is important."

Greffa smiled. Like her skin, her smile looked oily. "And the custom has been that the Giant's Thighbone takes the place of honor at the Jamboree. It has been so in my time. It was so in my mother's time and in my mother's mother's time and in my mother's mother's mother's time."

The Giant's Thighbone was the totem of the Barradik tribe, a huge, discolored artifact discovered in the days when Greffa's great-grandmother had sat on the elder council. It was larger than the bone of any animal except the mammoth, whose bones it did not resemble in the least. The Barradik claimed it was the thighbone of a giant who had lived in the dreamtime. They might, for all Renka knew, be speaking the truth.

But the truth of Barradik claims was not in dispute here. What was in dispute was *which* tribal totem should occupy the place of honor at the Jamboree. For as long as Renka could remember, that place had gone to the Giant's Thighbone of the Barradik. But this Star Year would be different. For now the Shingu held a totem far more marvelous, more powerful. Two years before, the Shingu orphan Shiva had discovered the Great Skull of Saber.

Renka nodded. "It has been so," she said solemnly. "Not merely through custom, but because the place was well deserved. There was no greater, more powerful, more magical totem than the Giant's Thighbone."

"Then you agree it should be the Star Totem again?" Saft put in, too impetuous as always—a characteristic which had probably caused her to be gored by the bull.

Renka allowed herself to smile, then shrugged. "It is not my place to say which totem should be chosen at the Jamboree." She paused, as if that were all she had to say, but added casually, "Although a greater totem than the Giant's Thighbone has now been discovered. . . ."

"This . . . thing the child found?" Greffa asked dismissively.

"The skull of a cave lion, isn't it?" Hai-line smiled sweetly. "I understand it is quite large."

It was not, of course, merely a question of honor. The tribe who provided the Star Totem at a Star Jamboree received gifts from every other tribe. And enjoyed huge prestige, for the totem was believed to contain the whole magic of the Jamboree for the following ten years. In this way the Barradik, who had provided the Star Totem for generations, had become one of the most powerful tribes in the land. They were not about to release their hold on that power without a fight. This meeting, Renka knew, was no more than the initial skirmish. She stared past the elders out of the cave mouth and across the rocky apron beyond. The hunter Hiram was squatted there, well distant from the cave, the bindings of one foot removed, picking nervously at his toenails. He had the look of one waiting for something terrible to happen.

Renka drew back her gaze, and looked directly at Hai-line. "It is the Skull of Saber, Hai-line." She leaned forward for emphasis. "Saber, the great cat who defied the Mother and was banished from the dreamtime."

Hai-line allowed one eyebrow to drift upward. "Really?" she said, her voice dripping disbelief.

"Really," Renka confirmed, smiling a little. She was neither worried nor concerned by these discussions. Before every Star Jamboree, each tribe put forward its claim to provide the Star Totem. But this was mere formality. In the past, the known totems could never measure up to something so unusual, so full of magic, as the Giant's Thighbone.

But the Shingu had the Skull of Saber now, and though the Barradik did not know it yet, the skull was genuine. The Crone had so pronounced it—not that, having seen it, anyone could have doubted its reality for an instant. The Skull of Saber would certainly displace the Giant's Thighbone as the Star Totem in the forthcoming Star Jamboree. Of that Renka had not the slightest doubt. Seeing both, no one would hesitate for an instant about which to select.

And Renka knew that when the Skull of Saber was selected, wealth, prestige and power would flow toward her tribe as rivers flowed toward the sea. Another chieftain might have welcomed the enhancement of her authority that this development would bring, but for Renka it meant only that the bad times would be over. No tribe that held the Star Totem ever went hungry.

"Perhaps," Greffa suggested sweetly, "we might be permitted to see this miraculous skull . . . ?"

Renka resisted an urge to glance toward the Crone. "I'm afraid," she told Greffa firmly, "that will not be possible."

"Not possible?" asked Greffa.

"Not possible?" echoed Hai-line.

"Not possible?" exclaimed Saft, her voice rising.

The Barradik warriors moved uneasily, sensing the discomfort of their elders.

"Why is it not possible?" Greffa asked, recovering her composure. Despite her oily manner and flabby appearance, she was not chief of the Barradik for nothing. She had a mind as sharp as freshly chipped flint. The look in her eyes told Renka instantly she now knew this was no commonplace negotiation where the Barradik would bribe away the rival claim. She was not quite certain—it might still be a clever ploy—but Greffa was coming to suspect that for the first time in living memory, the Giant's Thighbone might have a truly serious contender as the Star Totem.

Renka said, "The Skull of Saber is being prepared to take its place at the Star Jamboree." She paused for a single heartbeat, then added, "Magically prepared."

Greffa remained silent, but Saft was so lost to the subtleties of the situation that she began to shout, "Being prepared? Who is preparing this preposterous bone?"

"I am," hissed the Crone's dry voice from the shadows, so full of menace that even Renka shivered.

3
Hiram's Marriage Plans

Hiram waited nervously. It seemed to him he spent a great deal of his life waiting nervously for one thing or another. Years before, he had waited nervously for his initiation as a hunter. Then he had waited nervously when his mother, Sheena, had decided to instruct him in the mysteries of the Sacred Drums. Once he had even waited nervously to tell the elders how he had seen monstrous ogres prowling beyond their forest home.

He had never waited quite so nervously as now. Would Renka give permission?

Hiram was afraid of the tribal chief just as he was afraid of most women. But that did not matter, because he was forced to deal with women every day. The council of elders was composed of women. The leader of the Shingu hunt was a woman. Even his own mother was important, as Keeper of the Sacred Drums. There was no escaping women, so a young man like Hiram simply had to hide his fear and deal with them as best he could.

His stomach rumbled.

He glanced nervously toward the cave mouth. The Barradik elders looked peculiar with their purple faces, and their chief, he thought, looked positively repulsive. But he quite liked the way the warriors stuck feathers in their hair and painted themselves yellow. Perhaps it was a fashion he should adopt. The Barradik were a powerful tribe. If he stuck feathers in his hair and painted himself yellow, the women of his own tribe might take him more seriously. The young women, that was. Well, one young woman, anyway. The older women and the elders had always ignored him, more or less. As, admittedly, they ignored most young men. Although in his case, he had been especially ignored since his two disasters. He did not want to think about his two disasters.

He found himself thinking about his two disasters. The first had occurred when he discovered a sacred grove of marula trees, a magic grove, touched by the Mother Goddess herself. Which was not a disaster, of course. The disaster was when he became confused by the powerful magic in the grove and was unable to find it again. The tribe had followed him for days before he admitted defeat. No one said anything, no one laid blame, but Hiram knew the women thought he was a liar. He suspected they would think he was a liar till the day he died. He shuddered. It had been an enormous disaster, although not such an enormous disaster as the second disaster. He did not want to think about the second disaster.

He found himself thinking about the second disaster. Like the first, the second disaster had arisen out of triumph. He had seen the hideous ogre band, the monsters who ate children and were the sworn enemies of humankind. And because he had seen them, the elder council voted that he should lead the warriors against them. What a chance to prove himself! What an opportunity for fame and glory! Had he led a successful raid against the monsters, he would never have been ignored again by the elders. He would forever have been taken seriously by the young women—especially one particular young woman.

And what had he done? He had got himself captured by the ogres!

Even now he could scarcely believe his own stupidity. It had happened close by the encampment. One monster had seized him, held him helpless.

Then it and two other ogres had dragged him to that hideous ogre lair in the dark forest. If his tribe had not followed and rescued him, he would be dead. And eaten.

What young woman could take seriously a hunter who had almost been digested?

Shiva could, his mind whispered.

Shiva, Hiram thought fondly, was different. Although she was much younger than he, still a child and not yet a woman, somehow he found it difficult to think of her as a child. He had always found it difficult to think of her as a child, even years ago when she was much more definitely a child than she was now. She had always seemed so self-assured, so competent. She had always seemed so—he searched desperately for the right word and eventually found it—so still. There was a stillness about Shiva that was calming, relaxing, different from the other children who ran about like lunatics, different even from the young women—the pretty young women—who smiled at him and made him blush.

It was silly, but he felt safe with Shiva. And besides, she had taught him to see.

That was the heart of it, of course. Shiva looked at the world so very differently from others of the tribe. Once she had shown him a sunrise; and dawn had never been the same for him again. Once she had given him a flower; and now he saw flowers in a way he never had before. Shiva could make pictures in her mind, like a Crone, and Hiram, with much effort, found he could make pictures dimly too.

It had come upon him suddenly, the way so many important things did, that he wished to marry Shiva. Not now, of course, not right away. She was much too young for marriage yet. But in a year or two, when she became a woman—she could marry then. But he was terrified the husband she would take would not be him.

As a hunter, Hiram knew the importance of decisiveness and speed. The first to reach the herd had the pick of the game and often made the best kill. If he could tell Shiva now that he was willing— even anxious—to become her husband, then there was an excellent chance she would select him when the time came, because he had been the first to ask!

It was a good plan, simple and effective. But it had one important drawback. It went against custom.

No man in the tribe ever told a woman he wished to marry her. The custom was he waited until asked. He might refuse, of course—that was his right. But custom decreed that he waited. How, then, could he ever tell Shiva he wished to marry her, let alone tell her now before she had reached marriageable age? He had considered the problem for more than a week and reached the conclusion there was only one solution. He must ask permission of the chief to take this step against tradition.

Could Renka possibly give permission? He glanced toward the cave, hoping for some sign the meeting might be drawing to a close.

Even at this distance, it seemed there might be trouble in the cave. The Barradik elders were on their feet now, gesticulating, their purple faces darkened by a flush. Their warrior men had stepped back and were looking about them uncertainly. Hiram felt a surge of emotion that swept away his anxiety. Did the Barradik threaten Renka? But Renka still squatted calmly, her face as impassive as if she were discussing the storage of meat from a successful hunt. Besides, although he could not see her in the gloom of the cavern, he knew the Crone to be there. Renka needed no further protection than the magic of the Crone.

All the same, Hiram moved nonchalantly closer to the cave. Guided by his hunter's instinct, he slid into the shadow of a bush at the edge of the rock apron. From this new vantage point, the voices carried.

The Barradik Saft, whose mouth was permanently distorted by a hideously puckered scarring of both cheeks, was shouting, "You want more, don't you? You think this nonsense will make us give you more?"

The Barradik Hai-line, also on her feet, leaned forward so she towered over Renka. "This is a dangerous game, Shingu," she spat viciously. "The Barradik make bad enemies."

Hiram felt the hairs of his neck bristle, but despite the appallingly bad manners of her guests, Chief Renka remained calm. "Enemies?" she asked Hai-line quietly. "Why do you speak of enemies? Better you should listen to your chief, who mentioned custom. Is it not custom that each tribe may offer a totem at the Jamboree? Is it not custom that the most powerful totem is chosen?" She blinked, her face a vision of bland innocence. "And does this custom not benefit all the tribes, Barradik and Shingu and Tomara, the Karunbara and Lees and all the rest alike? Is it not the way in which we are all protected by the greatest magic?" She looked from one purple face to another, as if she expected an answer.

"Your totem skull is not yet judged," said Chief Greffa, holding her temper better than the others. "The Hag has not yet made her pronouncement."

Hiram shuddered at the name. The Hag was the Crone of Crones, the witches' elect, most powerful sorceress in the whole world. He had never seen her, but rumor had it she was old beyond imagining and more powerful than the god of lightning. She could slaughter a buffalo by the power of her will and turn a spear thrust on her naked breast, however strong the warrior who wielded it. The current Hag was of the tribe Menerrum—or possibly the Labo: Hiram could not quite remember— but for the Hag, tribe did not matter. As Crone of Crones, she was beyond tribal loyalties, honored, welcomed and feared (how she was feared!) by all the tribes.

As Greffa said, it was the Hag who selected the Star Totem of the Star Jamboree, sniffing the magic of each artifact put forward, then delivering a verdict so final it could not be questioned by the greatest chief.

"Indeed, she has not," Renka agreed. "Neither on the Skull of Saber, nor on the Giant's Thighbone."

"So the Shingu still plan to enter this skull for judgment?" Greffa asked.

"Of course." Renka nodded.

"Then there is nothing more to be said," Greffa exclaimed angrily. She gestured to her colleagues, and all three purple-painted women swept from the cave. Caught by surprise, their warriors stared after them for a moment, then collected their wits and followed.

Hiram watched their departure as renewed nervousness swallowed up his anger. He was still annoyed by the affront the Barradik had offered his chief. As everybody knew, the Barradik had always been ill-mannered. However, Chief Renka did not seem disturbed; and Hiram himself had more important things to concern him at that moment.

Would Chief Renka be prepared to let him break the ancient custom?

He watched as she emerged from the cave. She was actually smiling, which seemed to him a good sign. The Crone remained within, which was a gift from the Mother Goddess herself, for Hiram would never have found the courage to ask Renka anything in the presence of the Crone. He took a deep breath and stepped forward.

"Chief Renka," he began, "it is necessary that I ask you something of great importance—"

Renka looked at him benignly. She seemed in that instant almost carefree, like a hunter who has made a great kill or a warrior who has won a great victory. Her eyes sparkled, her face positively beamed with pleasure. She reached out and gripped his upper arm, shaking it lightly as a mother will sometimes do in order to placate a tiny child. "Not now, Hiram," Renka said. "I have urgent things to do."

Hiram watched her retreating back, square shouldered beneath the boarskin she wore so often. His mouth opened and shut of its own accord, but he could never have called her back. His mind ran around in tiny circles. What was he to do now?

Who knew what urgent matters Chief Renka had to attend to following her discussions with the Barradik? More importantly, who knew how long those important matters might take? A day, a week, a month? Who knew? And while those matters were attended to, might not Shiva decide to marry someone else?

An insane sense of urgency had gripped him so firmly that he could not shake it off. He had to tell Shiva that he wished to be her husband when the time came; and he had to tell her now!

As Hiram stared toward the spot where Renka disappeared from view, he did something he had never done before. Nothing outward showed, but inwardly Hiram mutinied. A decision hit him with the full force of an avalanche. What if it went against custom? *He would tell Shiva now how he felt!*

His heart began to pound at his own daring. When had he ever ignored custom? When had he ever found the courage to speak to any girl about his feelings? Yet he would do it. He knew he would do it—and now.

Where to find Shiva? He glanced sunward to estimate the time. She might be with the children— the little children had always been fond of her, although children her own age tended to avoid her. Or she might be doing some task, for she was a conscientious worker. But at this time of the day, she was more likely to have gone to the water hole—he had noticed her go there more and more often in the past few months.

The thought at once became a certainty. She had gone to the water hole. She had gone to the water hole and he would follow. He would follow and tell her how he felt. And to the nightwing with custom!

His emotions in a turmoil, Hiram trotted from the village, heading north.

4
Accused

She was not sure what to do. Light though the body was as she had pulled it from the water, Shiva did not think she could carry it back to the Shingu encampment—nor could she decide if she should. The old woman was not of her tribe, no business of hers, no business of her tribe, so why try to bring her back to the camp, risking the possibility that her spirit would follow?

And if she were to bring the body back to the camp, how would she manage it? There was something repulsive at the thought of dragging the remains of this old woman across tracts of ground that were sometimes muddy, always rough and stony. Her spirit would surely protest at such ill treatment. Yet Shiva did not think she could manage to carry the corpse for more than a short distance.

At the same time, she could not leave it here. Her nostrils told her that the cats were gone, but there would be other predators, less fastidious about carrion. Once Shiva left, the scavengers would arrive the moment she was out of sight. Even birds and rats would do considerable damage if nothing larger came by. The poor old woman had already lost her eyes to something in the pool. By the time Shiva returned to her village, reported her find and perhaps led a party of women back here, who could tell how much of the body would be left?

Shiva stared at the corpse, wondering who she had been. So old. So very old that it was almost impossible to believe any human being could have lived so long. What had she done, this old woman? Was she an elder of her tribe? Or just a favored grandmother who made herself useful by gathering nuts and grubs like the children? And what of the scarring on her back? That scar pattern had been placed there for a purpose, to mark her in some special way, as warriors were marked with paint when they were initiated into a lodge. Above all, how should Shiva deal with her body? Was it important? Did it matter?

The imaginary figure Shiva always called her mother (the mother who died in childbirth giving Shiva life) appeared by her side unbidden. "It matters," Shiva's mother said; and she disappeared again.

It mattered. Of course it mattered. Not because the woman was young or old. Not because she belonged to this tribe or that tribe. Not even because she was dead. It mattered because she had been murdered!

And there it was, the truth Shiva had striven to avoid, now hanging ominous and glittering in the forefront of her mind. This old woman had not been mauled by a lion or seized by the nightwing. She had not fallen from a cliff, or starved or faded from existence because of some disease. She had been killed by humankind, by one from among the many tribes, her skull crushed like an eggshell by a vicious blow with a heavy club. This was murder—and if death was always familiar, murder was not.

What to do? She must hide the body, protect it somehow from the scavengers; then, when the body was safe, she must run as fast as she could to the village camp and there tell Renka or some other elder. They would decide what was to be

34

done. Once she carried back the news, for Shiva the problem would be over.

She looked around. To keep a body safe from predators, even for a relatively short space of time, was not so easy as it sounded. The rock she had recently climbed would be useless: The body would be exposed to every bird that flew. To conceal it in the undergrowth would be even worse: There were so many things there that skittered and crawled and would welcome a feast of ancient flesh.

What she needed, Shiva thought, was a rock cleft or small cave—something with a narrow entrance she could easily block off once the body was inside. The taboos of the tribe forbade her (and any other Shingu) to enter a cave alone, a sensible ruling since so many caverns sheltered lions, bears, or ghosts. But in this instance, the sort of cave she sought would be too small, too shallow to hide anything particularly dangerous. Besides, since she had found the Skull of Saber, she was seldom seriously chastised by any of the tribe, whatever mischief she got into.

She looked around. A stretch of stony flatland led to the water hole from the east. Shrub surrounded it on the remaining three sides. But within the shrub to the north was a rocky outcrop, with a second close by.

She followed a game trail that led her to the first outcrop, but found neither cave nor crack nor fissure. She pressed on to the second, forced to push her way through thorny bushes, scratching the exposed portions of her legs. But this rock too was featureless—no safety for the old one's body there.

Disconsolately, Shiva returned to the water hole; and because she now approached it from an unaccustomed direction, she noticed for the first time a shadow (partly hidden by a bush) near the base of the rock on which she had lain to observe the cats.

She approached it cautiously, half wondering, half hoping, and saw at once it might be what she needed. Behind the bush was an opening.

Shiva moved slowly, sniffing. It was difficult to judge the size of a cave from the outside. This entrance was narrow, but that signified little, for it might widen in the darkness within to create a den for a bear or something else.

She smiled at her own foolishness. Whatever else might live beneath the rock, it would not be a bear. Even thinned by the long winter sleep, no bear could squeeze through the entrance. But a cat could. Not the huge cave lions, but certainly one of their smaller sisters. She had no desire to wriggle through the entrance and find herself face to face with a wildcat or a lynx.

She was close to the opening now and there was no smell of cat, no smell of any animal. All the same, she stood quite still and listened. There was the sighing of the wind, the call of the birds, the endless rustle of life, but nothing—nothing she was certain—from the cave.

Shiva took a deep breath and pushed the protective bush to one side.

This was always the time of greatest danger, for if anything did lurk within, this was the time when it would hurl itself forward to protect its home. But there was still no sound, still no hint of odor on the air.

She had done all she could. Nothing except fear was to be gained from waiting. She dropped down on one knee, pushed forward and squeezed head-first into the darkness.

Nothing seized her, nothing touched her. As her eyes grew accustomed to the gloom, she saw she was in a cleft little more than eight feet deep, narrow and low, inhabited by nothing more destructive than a few sleepy spiders. It was perfect to protect the old woman's body.

Shiva wriggled out again. She stood up and trotted over to where the old one lay. She took one wrist, thin as a dried-up twig, to lift this frail little remnant across her shoulders, ready to carry her the short distance to the cleft.

The old woman was even lighter than she had imagined, weighing little more than a child. Shiva stumbled with the body spread across her shoulders, but recovered and carried it easily enough the short distance to the opening. Gently she set it down again, pushed the bush to one side and eased the body through the narrow opening.

As she did so, some sixth sense froze her into immobility. Slowly she straightened and looked behind her. Only yards away was a yellow-faced warrior in wolfskins, black feathers stuck into his hair, a fire-tempered spear in his right hand. Beside him was another, and another, and another ranged in a rough semicircle. Shiva's eyes flickered from one to the other. She was surrounded.

The warriors stared at her silently.

"Who are you?" Shiva asked at once, knowing enough to hide her fear. How had they come so close? No hint of their scent had reached her, no sound of their approach had pricked her ears. They were skilled, these warriors. She wondered to which of the tribes they belonged. She knew there were many other tribes, of course, but was too young to have had much direct experience with them and could not yet read the signs.

A woman pushed forward, dressed and painted like the men but without the feathers in her hair, obviously their leader. "I am Weaver of the Barradik. What is your name and tribe, girl?" She had the sharp, confident tone of one accustomed to obedience. Perhaps she was an elder.

"I am Shiva," Shiva said. "My tribe is the Shingu." She was about to add that their encampment was nearby, but thought better of it and was silent.

One of the men, a flat-faced fellow with a portion of his right ear missing, whispered something to the woman.

"What have you hidden in the cave, girl?" Weaver asked.

Shiva said nothing. She disliked the way the woman called her "girl" even after learning her name. She disliked the arrogance in the woman's tone and in the stance of the men. In short, although this was the first time she had met any of its representatives, she disliked the Barradik tribe. And feared them.

The woman Weaver gestured and one of the men pushed Shiva brusquely to one side. He was too broad in the shoulder to squeeze through the cleft, but his eyes were keen enough to see despite the gloom. "Looks like a body in here, Weaver. Small body—a woman or a child."

Weaver's eyes widened. "What is in there, girl?" Her tone, never pleasant, had taken on an icy edge of menace.

"An old woman," Shiva muttered sullenly. The men were ranged a few feet apart. She wondered if she could dash through one of the gaps between them to escape. With surprise she might manage it.

"I can't hear you!" Weaver snapped.

"An old woman," Shiva repeated, more loudly this time.

"Dead?"

"Yes."

As if anticipating her thoughts, the warriors moved forward, closing the gaps.

"Why were you hiding her in the cave?" Weaver asked coldly.

Shiva lapsed back into silence. Some of her earlier fear was draining away, replaced by a growing anger. What right had this woman to question her? She was not even Shingu.

"Perhaps she murdered her," the flat-faced man suggested. He grinned.

"Did you kill her?" Weaver asked soberly. "Is

that why you were trying to hide her in the cave?"

"No!" shouted Shiva, shocked.

"There's blood on her club," the flat-faced man remarked. His smile had dropped away, as if he was considering his own suggestion seriously for the first time.

Shiva looked down, her fear suddenly grown large again. "That's *jackal* blood!"

The warrior by the cleft reached in and began to pull the old woman's body out by one ankle.

"Maybe it is and maybe it isn't," said the flat-faced man, referring to Shiva's claim that the blood was jackal blood.

The body emerged into the light and Weaver stepped forward to inspect it. As she bent forward, Shiva heard the inadvertent gasp of horror.

"Mother Goddess!" Weaver exclaimed. Blood drained from her face. She stepped back so quickly, she stumbled and would actually have fallen had not a warrior caught her arm.

"What's the matter, Weaver?" the man asked.

"It is the Hag!" Weaver gasped. "This girl has killed the Hag!"

5

The Tellstones' Secret

The entrance to the cavern was guarded. A broad-shouldered hunter squatted on either side, armed with spear and club. They bowed their heads in unison.

The Crone nodded briefly and passed between them into the gloom of the huge, high-roofed cavern. The floor was lightly strewn with rushes, gathered in their season and carefully dried in the small warmth of the sun. How much of her life, she thought without regret, had been spent in gloom.

How much of her adult life, she corrected herself. As a child she had enjoyed the light as much as any other, turned her young face toward the bright sky and played in freshly fallen snow. Her familiarity with passages and caverns began with her initiation as a witch. Only then had she begun to walk in darkness. It was a long life spent in darkness.

But of course there had been compensations.

She walked diagonally across the cave until she reached an opening in the far left wall leading into a narrow passage, which the light from the cave entrance failed to penetrate. She was dressed (since she had work to do) in the furred skin of a cave bear, so dark it was almost black, and she carried no torch or tinder or firebow.

The Crone stopped by the passage, sighed deeply once, then closed her eyes. She allowed her shoulders to droop, her muscles to fall limp as she called upon the inner vision.

Her inner vision worked equally well in darkness and in daylight. Thus, like all Crones with the second sight, she could find her way in blackest night without a flame of any sort. Eyes still closed, she stepped forward into the passage.

It was difficult going. The passage plunged downward, became narrower. Behind closed lids, her eyes flickered to and fro as if watching a dream. Familiarity guided her as much as her strange vision, and while she moved slowly, she moved surely. Eventually she reached several natural steps leading into a long, low-ceilinged gallery, which forced her to bend her head before she could proceed.

The gallery led to a second tunnel, wider and flatter than the first, but twisting. The tunnel opened onto a narrow ledge, which ran alongside a sheer drop of almost thirty feet. Eyes still closed, the Crone moved on without the slightest hesitation, neither speeding up nor slowing down as she negotiated the ledge.

The final passage ran straight and true and opened into a vast, multilevel cavern. The Crone opened her eyes at last. Often the cavern was in darkness, but at this time of the year the sun rose high enough to send illumination down a narrow, natural chimney so that here, for an hour or two each day, she could see with her physical eyes.

Not that sight was really needed. She could feel the painted images all around her, vibrant and true in her memory as much as in reality, crowding every surface of the rock. She allowed her eyes and mind to dwell on those magic pictures. She saw hunters, blessed so that they might more easily kill game. She saw a great mammoth, cursed so that it might be trapped in a pit. She saw the paintings that influenced the elk and the bison and the deer and the goats and the vast herds of auroch cattle.

Some of these images she had painted herself, first creating the pictures in her mind, then throwing them outward onto the rock and coloring them with pigments daubed by skillful fingers. But most were the work of Crones long gone, her sisters in sorcery ranging back to ancient times. She knew the style of every one.

From there she moved along the images and stopped at the strangest image of them all, the head of a great cat with fangs so large that they curved from his mouth like an elephant's tusks. Of all the paintings, this was the most vivid, its colors bright and new. She had created it herself, not two years before, in a burst of magic so intense she still had difficulty in understanding its nature.

She thought of that time now, of the threat to the tribe from the Forest Ogres sighted by the hunter Hiram, of the vision that had come to her as Crone. It was that vision that had heralded the magic. In it she had seen Saber, the cat who lapped from the Pool of Growth until he became so large he threatened the Mother Goddess herself and was banished from the dreamtime to roam the earth until he died.

It was Saber she had painted on the rock, the first time such a creature had ever been represented. It had been and still was her greatest magic.

It had prepared the tribe for war. It had ensured that the warriors successfully sought out the ogres. It had rendered the monsters temporarily powerless. And so profoundly did it influence reality that the orphan Shiva had been led to discover Saber's actual skull.

The Crone turned from her painting. Placed reverently on a natural rock altar, dimly illuminated by the filtered light, was the skull itself, a miracle made manifest. It was larger even than the skull of an adult male cave lion. And the curving fangs were far beyond those of any cat—or any other animal—she had ever seen. The Skull of Saber— already tribal totem of the Shingu, soon to be Star Totem of the Star Jamboree. How relentlessly the wheel of fate had turned from impending disaster to glorious triumph.

And the wheel still turns, a small voice warned within her mind.

The Crone stood still. She was an old woman; like most Crones, old beyond the natural span. Experience had taught her to listen to her voices— and never so carefully as when they spoke of things she had no wish to hear.

The wheel still turns.

She considered the phrase. Impending disaster to glorious triumph to . . .

To impending disaster? Was it possible the skull would not be chosen as Star Totem?

She examined the thought calmly. Possible, but difficult to believe. The Hag knew magic when she saw it. There had never been a totem so unusual, so strange, so full of power presented at the Jamboree. The Hag would not hesitate an instant in her judgment. Besides, although she was careful to conceal it, the Hag disliked the Barradik. She must have waited long for an excuse to refuse *their* totem.

And yet the wheel still turns. . . .

Alerted by the inner voice, the Crone's trained instincts asserted themselves at once. Her mind reached out like questing fingers, and she could feel menace in the air. But like her second sight, it was an outline without detail. Toward what or whom was the menace directed? She did not know. At least she did not know for sure. She found herself thinking of Shiva, the Shingu orphan girl who had found the skull. And suddenly the stench of death was in her nostrils.

Was it Shiva? Was Shiva threatened? Did death stalk the girl? The Crone had plans for Shiva, for the girl was more important than she knew. Where would disaster strike? How might it be averted?

The fear flowered fully in her breast and sent her

47

scuttling like a giant spider to a darkened corner of the cave. Too impatient to use second sight, she let her hands scrabble in the darkness until she found the package wrapped in soft doeskin. Ancient brown-spotted fingers unwrapped it of their own accord, raising the scent of herbs. Within was a strange assortment—scraps of fur and animal skin, dried plants, the wizened body of a lizard, leathery and old, knucklebones and polished, painted stones.

She separated out the stones and rewrapped the rest, setting them aside. Painted on one stone, the largest of her collection, was an eye, on another a clump of grass. Another showed the waves of the sea, another a star. She fingered two smaller stones, one painted with a sun, the other with a crescent moon. Beside them, on still more stones, were pictures of a flight of birds above a tree, crossed spears behind a shield, interlinked rings and finally a curving chipped flint blade.

Ten stones in all, the images on their surface far older and more crudely executed than any image on the cavern walls. These stones were the oldest things the Crone possessed, tellstones handed down from Shingu Crone to Shingu Crone, generation by generation, trailing back to the time when the Shingu hunted in the warm lands to the south and even the dreamtime was not far away.

She allowed her hands to play across them, forcing calm into her soul. Tellstones were a magic not every Crone could use, a special magic created for the few. Each stone had meaning; and though the meaning of each stone changed in accordance with its placement near another stone, still the meanings were easily learned.

What was not so easy was to forget them. For the real secret of the tellstones lay in the Crone who used them, not in the stones themselves. The Crone who used them (if she was to use them successfully) had to know deep in her heart when to accept a stone's meaning and when to reject it. It was a difficult skill, requiring much practice. But once achieved, it permitted a Crone to touch the stones and finger the very threads of destiny. It permitted her to look—a little way, at least—into the future.

What danger threatened Shiva? Was death walking by her side? Or was there something else, more sinister, more far-reaching?

Squatting in the gloomy cavern, the Crone scooped up the stones and threw them to create the mystic pattern. They clicked and clattered loudly as they struck the rock.

6

The Barradik Plot

The full council of the Barradik tribe numbered more than fifty members, but not all were equally important. In the front rank, where the real authority was vested, were only seven women. Three of these were the elders who had wasted their time in the futile attempt to bribe the stubborn Shingu—the Barradik chieftain Greffa and her cronies Hailine and Saft. The remaining four were Tooma, Lob, Sambaline and Orani, each representative of a powerful family in the intricate social structure of the Barradik tribe.

It was these seven who met now, not in the central council chamber but in a small, unmarked yurt on the periphery of the encampment. Outside, a party of five warrior males squatted in a tight clump playing a subdued game using polished knucklebones. The game was popular among the tribes and it did not look as if the men were guarding the yurt, but they were. This secrecy was typical of the inner council.

"So?" asked Sambaline. She was a slim, dark woman with the narrow eyes and prominently folded lids characteristic of her tribe. Some said she had ambitions to be chief, although she took care to support Greffa in public.

"It was as I thought," said Greffa sourly.

"She refused our gifts?"

"Arrogantly," Saft snorted. Although her puckered mouth gave her a permanent expression of surprise, her tone said clearly there was nothing unexpected about the outcome of their trip.

"But you saw the skull," Sambaline prompted.

Greffa shook her head. "We saw nothing."

"She refused you?" Sambaline's face expressed depths of disbelief. "Is the woman mad? Does she not recognize the insult?"

Greffa sighed. "Renka met us civilly enough." And she had. The Shingu were a small, insignificant tribe (or had been insignificant until now, she reminded herself sourly) led by an undistinguished woman. Of course the chief and elders of the mighty Barradik had been treated civilly. Throughout the entire discussion, Renka had been deferential and polite. But when it came to any point of importance, she had given nothing and revealed less. To Greffa that meant only one thing: The rumors were true—the Shingu held the actual Skull of Saber, or thought they did. It was the only thing that made sense of Renka's behavior. She would not have dared anger the Barradik otherwise.

"If you did not see the skull," said Lob, a solid woman whose thoughts seemed to move at a relentless pace, "then we cannot be sure they have it."

"No," Hai-line admitted, "but I think we must assume they do."

"And that it is genuine?" asked Tooma.

"It is genuine enough." Greffa sniffed. "Have I not said from the start that they had it and that it was genuine?"

"Their Crone vouched for it," put in Saft.

There was a sudden silence in the yurt. Small and insignificant though the Shingu tribe might be, it had been many years since anyone of any tribe had underestimated the Shingu Crone. The woman's powers were sinister, even for a Crone; and she had shown, on occasion, she was prepared to use them as ruthlessly as a she-bear defending cubs. Since the last Star Jamboree, it had been certain she would be the next Hag when the time came.

52

Not even the Barradik would have cared to field a candidate against her.

The silence held. Smoke from the central fire twisted upward to escape through a small hole in the funnel roof, a Barradik sophistication not seen in other tribes. Then Orani turned to one side and spat. "Their witch might be lying."

"I doubt it," Greffa said. "But in any case, I agree with Hai-line. We must assume they have the skull and that the skull is genuine. Any other assumption would be very dangerous to our interests."

"So what do you propose to do about it?"

Greffa stared at Sambaline, her face carefully composed. The woman was painfully thin, although food was never scarce among the Barradik. Greffa mistrusted thin women—at least thin women in positions of authority and power. She had always found them devious and often treacherous as well.

Before Greffa could answer Sambaline's implicit challenge, Tooma put in, "Is it certain they will not withdraw their totem?"

"Oh yes." Greffa nodded. "Quite certain. It will be submitted with the others at the Star Jamboree."

"And if it is genuine, the Hag will select it as Star Totem." This from Sambaline, her face impassive.

Greffa nodded silently.

"What do we know about the skull?" Orani asked.

Greffa glanced at Hai-line, whose hunters had gathered much of the information they already had about the new Shingu totem. She gave an almost imperceptible nod.

"The thing was found by a Shingu orphan called Shiva," Hai-line said. "In some sort of disused lair or cave."

"I thought the Shingu were afraid of caves," Tooma said.

"Entering caverns is one of their taboos. Entering them alone, that is. The only one supposed to do it is their Crone."

"Then how did this child get into the cave?"

"By accident," said Hai-line shortly. "I believe she was being chased—by an auroch or an elephant or something of that sort. She fell into the cave."

"If it was an auroch, she was very lucky to escape alive," murmured Saft, fingering the scar on one cheek.

"Did she know what she had found?" This from Orani.

Hai-line shrugged. "She knew she had found something of importance. Everything we have heard suggests the skull is very large and very strange to look at. I doubt she realized it was Saber's skull—she was only a child, after all. But she knew enough to bring it back to her tribe. The elders decided it must be the Skull of Saber."

"And their Crone confirms it," Greffa murmured.

Sambaline shifted her position as if to ease a cramp and said smoothly, "All this was more than two years ago. Why have we left it so late to consider taking action?"

Sweet Sambaline never missed an opportunity, Greffa thought. Someday soon she was going to have to deal with the woman. But Hai-line answered easily enough:

"The whole story has been wrapped around with all sorts of mystifications. The skull was supposed to contain so much magic, it gave the little girl power over ogres just by touching it. And it led one of their young men to a marula grove. And so on. You know how the small tribes always make up stories to glorify themselves—"

"And the Shingu have always been notorious liars." Saft snorted.

"—So for a long time we did not take any of it seriously," Hai-line went on. "Even now it is quite difficult to sift the facts from the nonsense."

"I didn't know the Shingu still believed in ogres," Tooma remarked. "I didn't know *anybody* still believed in ogres."

"But in all the nonsense, there is still the hard fact of the skull itself—is that not so?" Sambaline asked.

Hai-line nodded. "Oh yes. Evidently a skull exists. It has been officially adopted by the Shingu as their totem. I don't know if it is the actual Skull of Saber, but by all accounts it is certainly a very large, very strangely formed skull."

"Which the Hag is likely to select as Star Totem over our Giant's Thighbone," Sambaline said harshly.

It was time, Greffa thought, to put the skinny upstart in her place. "Even the Hag may think twice about incurring the displeasure of the Barradik nation," she said firmly.

"I don't see why," said Sambaline. "She never has before."

"Maybe this time we should not worry too much about the Hag," Saft said mysteriously, and giggled.

"The point," said Greffa heavily, "is not what the Hag may do, but what we should do. That is the purpose of this meeting."

"So far," Sambaline said, "what we have done doesn't seem to have made much difference."

"What we have done so far is find out information," Greffa spat. "That is all. Remember, Sambaline, I was the one who said long ago the Shingu had a skull, and I was the one who said they would not accept our gifts. We had to try, we had to make the offer, but let us not pretend the situation has developed any differently from the way we thought it would. What we have to decide now—without bickering—is what to do next."

"What to do next?" echoed Sambaline. "What *can* we do next?"

Greffa smiled coldly. "One possibility," she suggested softly, "would be to *steal* this Shingu skull."

There was total silence for a moment. To her credit, Sambaline made no pretense at shock—as a group they had discussed much worse than theft on past occasions.

"An interesting possibility," Sambaline began thoughtfully. "Provided, of course, that we move quickly. The Jamboree is only—"

But a commotion outside drowned her final words. Greffa looked across at Saft. "Find out what is going on!" she ordered sharply.

"Yes, Greffa," Saft said obediently, and scuttled from the yurt.

7
Hiram Hunts

Hiram fell without thought into the hunter's trot, a stride that was not particularly fast but still ate distance, since it could be kept up, mindlessly, mile after mile, without exhaustion. It also permitted him to follow a trail while moving quickly, as long as it was fresh and reasonably obvious. The trail he followed was that laid down, unwittingly, by Shiva.

It was a trail composed of tiny, separated signs: a tuft of gray-brown wolf fur from the skin she wore, caught on a thorn, the curving edge of a footprint set in icy mud, the split pulp of kreta fruit without its seeds (Shiva loved the taste of kreta seeds), a broken branch at the height of Shiva's shoulder. All told their story clearly to a hunter, the more so because she had made no attempt to hide her trail. The trail led, as he had thought it would, to the water hole.

He saw the signs of the great cats before he reached it, far sooner than Shiva had picked up their scent. It spoke well of his hunter's eye that he was only momentarily confused, for the cats were of even weight and it would have been easy to assume there had been only one. But the left hind foot of one feline had scarring on the pad, and this he noticed. The shape of the tracks, on soft ground, told him they were lions; the depth, that they were probably lionesses. Farther on, he found tawny hair from a tail tuft, confirming his suspicion about the nature of the beasts, if not their sex. All the same, he was certain enough of their sex from the pattern of their tracks. They moved as hunters moved, and that meant females. Male lions are lazy. They liked to sit in caves all day until their mates brought back the meat.

A small thought gnawed like a mouse at a corner of his mind: Had Shiva avoided the lions? He pushed it away. Of course she had avoided the lions. She was always careful. Besides . . .

Hiram did not really want to think of this. But the thought, once begun, crawled over him of its own accord. Besides, he thought, Shiva would have been warned about the danger.

It was the only aspect of Shiva that made Hiram uneasy. For years now he had known she played and spoke with people others could not see. There were her father and her mother (both dead) and sisters she had never had and some strange breed of animals called wobbles. She told him she "made them up," created them in her mind, for fun. But Hiram knew these creatures sometimes warned Shiva when she was threatened, and how could that be if she created them in her mind? She could call him silly if she liked—as she once had, bluntly, to his face—but to Hiram there was only one answer. However much Shiva might deny it, she had the Crone's trick of speaking to spirits.

He managed to break away from the disturbing thoughts by invoking the excitement of what he planned to do. When he found Shiva, he would tell her he wished to be her husband. One day. One day soon. No, not soon, but one day. That is, if she wanted him.

He came to the water hole, disturbing a fox that had been drinking in the shallows. Shiva was not there.

He felt a momentary surge of disappointment, but dismissed it as unreasonable. He had expected to find her at the water hole, had tracked her to the water hole, but had simply *missed* her at the water hole. She would not be far away.

He frowned. But where was she likely to be? Shiva came to the water hole to drink or to wash— he was not sure which—then returned to the encampment. But if she was returning to the encampment now, why had he not met her on the way? Surely she would return by the same path she went?

He moved across the barren sweep that led to the water hole, searching for her sign. And as he reached the water hole itself, alarms were sounding in his mind. This was more than a niggling worry. Something was wrong. His keen gaze traveled around the area.

He saw a bush leaning to one side beneath the rocky overhang.

He saw an opening beyond.

He saw marks in the soil.

He saw a broken spider's web and behind it three broken branches on a bush.

He saw a black feather.

He saw scuff marks near the edge of the water hole itself, close by where the fox had been drinking, but not the marks—certainly not the marks— a fox might make.

He saw a smear of yellow ocher on a stone.

He saw the gray-brown hairs of Shiva's wolfskin clinging to a bush.

The separate signs came together in his mind and suddenly he saw, almost as clearly as if he had been present, what must have happened. Shiva at the water hole, drinking, washing—who knew? Warriors approaching, stealthy, silent, Barradik men with yellow faces and black feathers in their hair. An attack. A struggle.

The Barradik had taken Shiva!

Horror ran through his veins in place of blood. She was taken! They had taken his Shiva! And with the horror came the questions. Where had they taken her, these Barradik? Above all, why?

There was no enmity between the Barradik and Shingu. The tribes seldom warred and, with the exception of the northern Lees, seldom sought to. In this vast, cold land, each had its own hunting grounds and sacred sites. Even a large tribe like the Barradik might go for years without even meeting another tribe. One year in ten, there was a gathering of all tribes at the great Star Jamboree, but between times there was scarcely an opportunity to quarrel, let alone a motive.

Why had they taken Shiva? His mind dismissed a host of possibilities. The Barradik had no need of slaves or servants, even if the Crones had not forbidden the forcing of another's labor. Shiva had no wealth. She was an orphan. And besides, compared with the Barradik, the entire Shingu tribe was poor. Had she wronged them in some way? He could not imagine how. Why had they taken her? She was of no importance to the Barradik.

She had found the Skull of Saber.

He chilled at the thought. Shiva was important. The Mother Goddess had led her to escape a charging beast and find the Skull of Saber, the great cat banished from the dreamtime. Although she seemed no different, behaved no differently, from any other girl, Shiva had been chosen. Even the Crone had treated her with respect when she brought back the skull. And the ogres—he shuddered at the thought of those forest monsters and how close she had been to them. Yes, Shiva was different. Not rich, not powerful, but different. Perhaps this very difference made her important to the Barradik.

Where had they taken her? Hiram knew the tribes were gathering in this district in preparation for the great Star Jamboree, but custom dictated that it was impolite to spy, so he did not know precisely where anyone was camped. He suspected the Barradik might not be far off. Their chief, after

63

all, had visited his chief, Renka; and their chief was fat as well as ugly, obviously incapable of traveling any great distance. So they must be fairly close by. But where?

In a frenzy of impatience, Hiram hunted for a sign. And though it seemed as if he searched forever, only seconds went by before he found it. He followed the trail slowly until he was certain of its general direction, then broke once again into the loping hunter's trot. As he ran, he placed sign on sign in his mind. There were a number of Barradik, certainly more than eight and possibly more than twelve. From their tracks, only one was a woman, probably their leader. And Shiva was with them.

Their camp—if they were really taking her to their camp—was farther than he had imagined, and the trail led in an uncomfortable direction: toward the dark forest where the ogres lived. Even as he followed it, Hiram began to wonder if he was doing the right thing. Should he not have returned to his village camp and told the elders what he had discovered? Should he not have allowed them to take charge of the emergency, as was their right? He had no doubt they would have taken action, for, as he had just recently remembered, Shiva was important—she had been favored by the Mother

Goddess, led by the Mother to the cave of Saber's skull.

And if she had indeed been taken by the Barradik, would the elders not have negotiated for her return? Had he returned to the village, the whole power of the Shingu tribe would have turned toward achieving Shiva's return, even aided by the magic of the Crone. Yet here he was, tracking her captors alone. It was foolish to the point of madness.

Despite the thought, Hiram did not turn back.

8
The Trek

While the Barradik encampment was still somewhere beyond the distant horizon, a yellow-faced
runner appeared over the brow of the next hill.
Weaver called a halt at once and waited. Shiva
seized the opportunity to rest, her back against a
rock. She too watched and waited.

Shiva was afraid. The woman Weaver had spo-
ken no word to her throughout the entire journey
here, and the warrior men had handled her
roughly, shouting orders and jerking her arm to
ensure she kept apace with them. And a hard pace
they had set, but Shiva, who had had to make her
own way since childhood, gritted her teeth and
stayed. She was falsely accused and that was
enough. She would show no weakness. Thus she
hid her tiredness and her fear.

It was fear that did not altogether spring from her capture, or what she thought might happen to her. A large part came from what had already happened. The old woman was the Hag! Shiva still found it difficult to believe, although Weaver's horror had been real enough. But the Hag! The Crone of Crones. The witch to whom all witches bowed. Shiva had never seen the Hag in life, but like all in the tribes she knew her fearsome reputation. She had imagined someone like the Shingu Crone, but taller and more sinister, if that were possible. She could see nothing of her imaginings in that frail, tiny, ancient corpse.

Two of the warriors were carrying it between them, with enormous respect. They did not even set the body down now that a halt was called, but stood, nervously patient as beasts, carefully holding the body clear of the ground. Shiva did not doubt they knew the Hag's reputation equally as well as she. They had argued among themselves about touching the body, as if power and magic clung to it still. The flat-faced man with the injured ear had refused to touch it altogether. Only a direct order from Weaver persuaded the two who now carried it to take on the job; and even then they were reluctant.

The Hag murdered! Shiva shuddered at the sheer

enormity of the crime, the crime of which *she* now stood accused.

She pushed the thought from her mind. There was nothing she could do about the accusation, little she could do about her situation. The warriors watched her constantly, so there was no opportunity to attempt to escape. Nor, she thought, would she get far even if, somehow, she succeeded. They had been moving across the plains for some hours now, and while the flatland was not entirely featureless, there were still few places to hide. And her chances of actually outrunning the Barradik warriors seemed slim.

She stared at the ground beneath her feet, feeling the hardness of the rock against her back. Would there be help from her tribe? She thought there might. Renka was a fair, just and caring chief. But would Renka know? Who was there to tell her a Shingu orphan had been kidnapped by the Barradik? It might be a long time before she was even missed. She often went off on her own; and those who knew her best knew that.

The runner arrived, streaming sweat despite the cold. He made straight for Weaver, scarcely taking time to catch his breath. They were too far away for Shiva to hear what was being said, but she saw Weaver nod several times. Eventually she waved the man away. He did not leave but moved to join the warriors, who welcomed him.

Weaver signaled and the party, which had spread out a little during the waiting period, now re-formed into a tight group. One of the men jerked Shiva roughly to her feet, but she bit back her instinctive protest and only stared at him blankly. Then they were on the move again. But now they were on a different route, one that ran, for a time at least, almost at right angles to their original course.

They had traveled for another hour before she suddenly discovered why. As they crossed a ridge of high ground, she glanced to the west and saw there, in the distance, a huge herd of grazing mammoth, several hundred strong.

She stared and slowed her pace so much that a warrior poked her rudely as a reminder to keep up. She had seen mammoth before, but not often and never so many together at one time. Even at this distance they were enormous, lumbering giants with the ragged mottling of their woolly coats that summer always brought. Huge tusks curved and soared toward the sky.

On the edge of the herd, two bulls were head to head, apparently ready to do battle, trunks raised to trumpet challenges Shiva was too far away to hear. The Mother had promised the mammoth she should be the largest of all the animals; and so it was, despite the efforts of the great cat Saber. A herd was an awesome sight, and this herd grazed across the exact path the party had originally taken. Had Weaver continued the way she was going, they would have ended up in the middle of the giants.

Despite her desperate situation, Shiva found she was experiencing a small pang of regret that the runner had managed to warn them so soon. She would have liked to have seen so large a herd at closer range. And really there was little danger from mammoths unless you went too close. They ate only grass and vegetation and were so enormous that not even a lion pride would care to tackle an adult. From the corner of her eye she noticed the two sparring bulls had already lost interest in their disagreement and were wandering away to inspect some bushes. Then she dropped below the level of the ridge and the herd was out of sight.

She wondered how much farther she had to go.

No one had told her anything, but she assumed they were marching to the Barradik camp. What might happen when they got there was a contribution to her gnawing fear.

She thought she might be brought before the elders. That was certainly what would happen within the Shingu. But after that, she was far from sure. The Hag was dead—murdered. Shiva had been found hiding the body, with blood on her club. It was no surprise they thought at once of murder. The obvious accusation had already been made. But would the Barradik elders try her or send her back to her own people? She did not know; and those who had taken her would not say, would not even speak to her.

If she was returned to her own people, she would be safe. Renka and the elder council were fair, just women. They knew her. They knew she could never kill another human being. And they were wise. They would ask what gain there was for Shiva—or for any Shingu—in murdering the Crone of Crones. In Shingu law there was a maxim: No guilt without gain. When any Shingu was accused of crime, the elders first asked, *What profit was this crime to her?* And if the answer was *none*, then they held it unlikely that the accusation was well founded.

But supposing she was *not* returned to her own people? Supposing she was destined to face Barradik justice? There was the root that grew the

71

flower of fear. The Barradik were strangers to her. Who knew what rough justice she might receive at their hands?

There was so much she did not know, but one thing she knew too well. Wherever the trial, whatever the tribe, the penalty for murder stayed the same. In all the tribes, that penalty was death. If the Barradik thought her guilty, she would be taken to a high place and stoned until she died. No tribe, not even the Lees who had so many strange customs, would permit a murderer to live.

A certain familiarity in her surroundings impinged on her thoughts. She looked around, taking careful note of landmarks, and decided she had been in this area before. For a moment she could not quite remember when; then it came to her. She had passed this way when she and the ogre boy Doban had fled her village that strange night so long ago, fleeing from Shiva's own people, who had taken Doban prisoner. They had come by an unfamiliar route, but were surely approaching the dark forest that had been Doban's home.

"Keep up!" snarled the flat-faced man with the injured ear. He cuffed her with the back of his hand, not hard, but enough to make her cheek sting. Shiva swung her head around and glared at him and was surprised when he fell back a pace under the impact of her gaze. But he recovered quickly and waved a fist at her and shouted hoarsely, "Just mind your manners, girl, or you'll be in a lot more trouble!"

She wondered why he obviously disliked her so much. She wondered why he seemed to feel so nervous near her. She wondered what more trouble she could possibly be in when she was already accused of murder.

They came to a stretch of rocky ground, and the going slowed appreciably. Shiva noted she was not the only one who welcomed a respite from the grueling pace. Several of the warriors relaxed visibly, although Weaver's expression did not change: She seemed relentless as a rock.

At one point Shiva trod on a loose stone and stumbled against the flat-faced warrior who strode beside her. She felt him jerk away from contact as if she had been a snake with poison in her mouth. This was more than nervousness—the man actually feared her. Why?

One of her sisters appeared as a vision in her mind. *Because he really does believe you killed the Hag,* she whispered.

And the realization came upon her like a blizzard. Not just the flat-faced warrior—they all feared her, these Barradik. Even Weaver, who showed so little emotion, kept her distance. And the reason they feared her was that they genuinely thought she had killed the Hag!

Shiva suddenly saw herself as she must appear to them. Not a thin child from a different tribe, her wiry muscles wrapped in wolfskin. Not even a girl with blood on her club. If they believed she had killed the Hag, they believed her to be *magic*! For the Hag was sorcery incarnate, and only magic could kill magic.

At once she remembered all the stories she had heard about the Hag. The Crone of Crones oozed mystic power. She could slay buffalo with a touch. She could withstand a charging rhino—and Shiva, who had once been charged by a rhino herself, knew just how impressive that must be! She could turn a spear thrust on her naked breast. She could find game when the best hunter failed. She could recite the past and see the future and read the thoughts in women's hearts. Her arts made her more powerful than the greatest chief.

And they all thought Shiva, silent Shiva, Shingu orphan, had somehow killed her! No wonder the flat-faced warrior had fallen back from her glare. At once Shiva wondered how she might turn this realization to her own account. If they feared her so, might that not somehow make it easier for her to escape?

She was still wondering when they came upon the Barradik camp. The camp was like no village Shiva had ever seen. Instead of the familiar Shingu longhouses with their scattered circle of lean-tos there were row upon row of yurts, conical brown leather tents, all, as far as she could see, of similar size. Each was large enough to hold perhaps half a dozen adults in reasonable comfort.

And the encampment was huge. Shiva had thought the Shingu a large tribe—or at least a tribe of average size. Now, on the instant, she knew it to be small; and, in comparison with the Barradik, tiny. The yurts stretched endlessly across the plain, a veritable forest of tents, housing this most powerful of the tribes.

That power was indicated as much by location as by size. The site of the camp was open on three sides, unprotected by any natural feature. On the fourth, close by, was the dark forest, exactly as she had remembered it. No tribe in Shiva's knowledge would have dared camp so close to the forest, with its howling packs of timber wolves, its vicious boars, its moaning spirits and its ogre clans. No tribe, that was, except the Barradik, whose power

was so great they had nothing to fear. Their campsites were chosen for comfort and convenience.

Even from a distance, she could see scores of
warriors in the camp, yellow-faced and feather-
haired like those who surrounded her, prowling
the perimeter like beasts, spears bristling from their
hands. Among the Shingu people, warrior paint
was donned only in time of war, but the Barradik,
it seemed, wore it all the time.

There was another difference. Almost all the Barradik warriors were men, while among the Shingu
men and women were equally likely to be warriors,
although women were more likely to be leaders.
Men too tended the ringfires of the Barradik camp,
alight even now in daytime; and men, she saw,
were preparing carcasses of reindeer brought in,
presumably, by men from the Barradik hunt. In all
tribes save the northern Lees, women ruled, but in
the Barradik, it seemed, women ruled and did little
else.

A party of warriors marched out of the encampment to escort Weaver's party in. Shiva caught only
fragments of a brief exchange between Weaver and
the woman who led them and could make little of
it, although there were several glances in her direction.

Then the two parties blended and the warriors

surrounded her, and if they feared her, they took care not to show it. And all marched into that forest of yurts as word of what had happened spread like wildfire.

9

The Rescue Plan

Renka frowned. "Are you sure?"

The Crone regarded her soberly, black eyes glittering, and said nothing.

Renka shook her head helplessly. "Where? Who? *Why?*" She felt fearful and angry by turns, but at this point mostly angry. Her meeting with the Barradik chief had been a triumph and she had hoped to enjoy the feeling a little longer. Although it was no surprise that she could not: a chieftain's lot was one of constant problems. But Shiva taken? Who would take her? Not a Shingu, for Shiva was honored by the tribe since her discovery of Saber's skull. And if not a Shingu, to whom was she important? A thought occurred. "You don't mean taken by some animal?"

But the Crone shook her head. "No animal. The girl is taken by the Barradik."

The *Barradik*? Renka leaned forward and again hissed, "Are you sure?"

And this time the ancient witch nodded. "Yes. Even now she approaches the Barradik encampment."

They were alone in the longhouse, its fire burning low and in need of tending. Dried plants hung from the ceiling, stained with smoke. Renka leaned back and closed her eyes. The implications chased one another through her mind, none of them pleasant to contemplate. "Why?" she asked simply.

"I do not know, Leader," said the Crone. "I know only that she has been taken and is in danger." Her eyes misted briefly, then cleared. "Great danger."

"The skull—?"

"It is safe," the Crone confirmed.

It had to do with the skull, Renka thought. Of course it had to do with the skull. What other interest had the mighty Barradik in the poor Shingu? Even before the visit of their elders, Renka had thought the Barradik might try to steal the skull. But the skull was well hidden and well guarded, protected too by the enchantments of the Crone.

If not the skull, had they settled for the girl who had found it? They would know she had been favored by the Mother and like all such was a living totem of her tribe. Saft of the gored cheeks and puckered mouth was such a one to the Barradik and sat with the elders because of it. Shiva was too young to sit on any council, but was valued by the Shingu just the same.

The answer came to Renka on the instant. "They hold her hostage! They will demand the Skull of Saber in return for Shiva, who found it."

But the Crone shook her head again, slowly. "A hostage is of value only as long as she is kept alive. I have cast the tellstones. Death stalks Shiva like a hunting cat. There is death behind her, death beside her, death before her."

"Why would the Barradik wish her dead?" asked Renka softly.

"I do not know. I know only that the girl must die unless a Shingu saves her."

And there they were, the words Renka had most dreaded. She knew their truth, of course, had known their truth the moment the Crone had come to her. Shiva had been taken by the Barradik who wished her dead. Thus Shiva would die in Barradik hands unless the Shingu saved her.

80

But how could the Shingu save her? Renka had been chieftain of the Shingu for more years than she cared to dwell upon; she loved her tribe with the abiding intensity of a mother for her child. But for all her loyalty and love, she had never lost her sense of perspective. The Shingu were a small, impoverished tribe, insignificant among the other tribes. In many a winter, the Shingu hungered—and in some the Shingu died—because their weakness bound them to the poorer hunting grounds. Shingu women and Shingu men were hunters and providers. Only once since the last Star Jamboree had the Shingu donned the paint of warriors and danced the Dance of War. And even then the war had been averted.

All this Renka knew as well as she knew the far histories of her tribe. For such a tribe to move against the Barradik was madness. The Barradik were more numerous than grains of sand on a shore, more powerful than a mammoth herd, more wealthy than Hanrikki, the fabled beast who held the treasures of the dreamtime.

"We cannot move against the Barradik, Sister," Renka whispered softly. "In war they would kill our warriors and scatter our nation. The Shingu would become no more than a memory in the histories of the tribes."

"This is true," the Crone agreed. "We must proceed by stealth."

Renka waited. The Crone had woven her enchantments throughout all the years that Renka could remember, old, lined, changeless from the days when Renka was a girl. In all that time, her magic had protected, her wisdom guided the tribe. There had been leaders—Chana, Tanaranu and now Renka herself—but behind them loomed the brooding figure of the Crone. Her world was one of mysteries and spirits, dark caves and conversations with creatures others could not even see. She seldom interfered with the activities of the tribe and sat silent at the council, voicing an opinion only when consulted. But whatever she required of her people was given. Renka might be chief, but ultimate authority was vested in the Crone.

The Crone sighed. "A hundred Shingu could not rescue Shiva. One Shingu might."

"One?"

The Crone nodded. "If we select the right one."

"A man or a woman?" Renka asked.

"A woman. It would be foolish to entrust so important a mission to a man. But that woman must be of subtle mind, courageous, skilled and strong. Above all, she must be calm in the face of danger. She will wear the purple of the Barradik council."

Renka's mind jumped ahead on the instant. "You want one of our women to impersonate a Barradik *elder*?"

"Yes."

"It is not possible, Sister!" Renka gasped.

"It is possible," the Crone said calmly. "The Barradik are more numerous than you can imagine. There are fifty women on their council—*fifty*. And these change frequently. The tribe is ruled by Greffa and a few of her friends who remain at the center of things always, along with a handful of representatives from the most powerful families. But beyond this there are forty or more councilors whose faces change frequently as minor families jostle for power. A woman becomes an elder for a time, wields power, then is dismissed and replaced. Among the forty all is flux and change. It is not as it is among the Shingu, where everyone knows all. With the correct dyes and the correct clothing and the correct air of arrogance, our woman may pass for a Barradik elder for as long as she needs to."

"How long will that be?" Renka asked her bluntly.

"Long enough to enter the Barradik camp and

rescue Shiva." She held Renka with her eyes for seven silent heartbeats, then asked, "Will you undertake the task, Renka?"

Renka sat for a moment in stunned amazement.

Eventually the Crone repeated, "Will you undertake the task, Renka?"

Renka blinked. "I—of course—there may be another who would be better than—"

But the Crone cut in dryly. "This is a dangerous mission. I believe it to be necessary and I hope it will succeed, but I have no vision of its outcome. She who carries out this task must be the best and strongest of our nation. I have lived long and known, in total, four chiefs. You are the best of these, Renka—the best I have ever known. Thus you are the greatest of our tribe."

Renka swallowed, utterly unable to reply. She stilled the babble of her emotions, examined her own thoughts, then said with a modicum of calm, "I am known to the Barradik, Sister."

"You are known by sight to only three Barradik," the Crone said softly, "Greffa, Hai-line and that witless imbecile Saft. In a camp as large as that of the Barradik, it is unlikely that you will meet up with any of these three." She reached forward and threw a small piece of wood onto the dying fire. "But should you do so, you are still Renka.

You are still leader of the Shingu nation. Custom decrees that such a one as you shall not be harmed by those of another tribe, except in time of war. An orphan girl is one thing—a tribal chieftain quite another. How soon can you leave?"

"Soon," Renka said, still flustered. "At once—" She made a nervous gesture with her hands. "I don't even know where the Barradik are camped."

"Their yurts are raised beside the dark forest, near the small river we call Yarr," the Crone said promptly.

"I know the spot." Renka nodded, not pausing to wonder how the Crone knew the Barradik were there. She began to stand, then hesitated, her mind in turmoil. "There must be a plan, Sister. I must have a plan." She had no plan. Her thoughts would not function.

"I have your plan." The Crone leaned forward. "You will approach the Barradik encampment by night—"

"By night?" Renka echoed.

"It is the only way," the Crone said stonily. "Your greatest danger is your approach to the camp. That is when you are most likely to be questioned, most likely to be seen as a stranger. Once among the yurts, there are so many Barradik that you may mingle with them safely. The manner of your bearing, the purple of your face will discourage questions. You are accustomed to rule. It shows in your bearing. They will easily accept you as an elder. But there can be no question of an approach in daylight. You must enter the camp at night, with great stealth. The Barradik are not at war. Their sentries expect no attack and will be lax. Their ringfires are always well stocked. It will be a simple matter to get in. When you do, you must find where they are holding Shiva and rescue her."

So simple—it sounded so simple. "She will be guarded."

"Doubtless," the Crone said dryly. "But she will be guarded by Barradik men, who are the most foolish creatures in the world, with the possible exception of a hedgehog. You will be marked by the purple of a Barradik elder. You will order them to go away."

"But if they see through my deception?" Renka protested. "If they refuse to obey my order?"

The Crone seemed to lose patience for the first time. "Then you will kill them, Renka."

They sat staring at one another for a long time. The piece of wood the Crone had thrown on the fire blazed suddenly and sent shadows dancing.

"Even if I leave at once, it will take a full day's

march to reach the place. Will Shiva be safe until . . . ?"

The Crone shrugged. "Who knows? The child may die within the hour, may be dying at this very moment or already dead. We cannot guarantee to rescue her. We can do no more than try. But beyond that, I tell you here that you shall not spend a full day's march in reaching her. Walk with me, Renka." She stood and moved with easy grace out of the longhouse. Renka followed her at once.

They walked from the village, the Crone silent as a corpse. In a few minutes Renka realized they were approaching the hallowed area of sacred, tree-ringed ground where none might enter save by invitation of the Crone. As chieftain, Renka had visited the sacred ground before, yet still she slowed her pace.

"Stay by my side," the Crone said.

They passed among the trees and entered the grove. Within, grazing, was a piebald mare. To Renka's astonishment, it made no movement to run off at their approach.

10
Hiram Meets a Monster

It began to rain, one of those short, chill downpours that characterized the season. With the wind at his back, Hiram trotted on, his long hair quickly plastered to his skull and water streaming down to creep through every opening of his furs and skins. He scarcely noticed the additional discomfort. Discomfort was a way of life.

He did, however, notice that the countryside around him was beginning to take on a horrid familiarity. At first this reached him only as a feeling of unease, the sort of early-warning danger signal familiar to every hunter. But in this case the danger was long gone. As Hiram trotted on, he came to realize he was approaching closer to the spot where he had seen the ogres.

It had happened two years ago, before the river

changed its course, so the tribe was then camped at its old site farther north along the range of cliffs. And it had happened, as so much of importance in Hiram's life, because of Shiva.

Hiram had left camp early, in the confusing brightness of a false dawn, for no better purpose than to watch the rising sun. Later, when he reported his experience, quaking, to the elder council, no one understood what he had been doing. Doubtless they thought he had crept off to see some girl, for young men of Hiram's age thought of girls a lot. He had not even tried to explain. Without Shiva, it was impossible to explain.

On this occasion, however, he saw more than a sunrise.

Even now, over the gulf of years, he still shuddered at the horror of it. Shuddered even more so since he now realized it had all begun somewhere close by. On that distant morning, near this very place, he had seen his first real ogre.

Ogres had long been a part of tribal lore. They were creatures terrifying as the nightwing, ugly as a decomposing corpse. They were demons in rough human shape, but more hairy, more squat, more muscular, with fangs and evil eyes. They ate brains and babies.

Like many a young man who had been frightened by ogre tales in childhood, Hiram had not really believed in ogres when he became a man, although the tribal histories insisted there had been wars between the ogre clans and humankind right up to recent times.

But not even the oldest of the tribe could remember ever having seen an ogre. One or two told Hiram seriously that their grandmothers had been involved in ogre wars; and one even claimed his father had spotted one of the monsters on the day of his initiation into the Bear Lodge. Hiram listened politely, but declined to believe. Everybody's grandmother was the stuff of legend, and it was well known that initiation into the Bear Lodge involved consumption of a certain potion which made men very silly.

But then he had seen the ogres for himself.

There had been more than one. He thought he counted five, but there might have been four or six. The sight of them confused him. Hiram had never been a nervous child, and as a hunter he had proved his courage time and time again. Once he had even faced a charging buffalo to save two of his companions. But the ogres affected him as no animal, however dangerous, had ever done. He was so shaken he actually shook, fear vibrations thrilling through his body like leaves rustling in a winter wind. He was so frightened he wanted to moan with terror, but was too afraid to make a sound.

They were like the stories he had heard, yet quite unlike anything he had imagined. Somehow they were far more horrible. They were, as the legends told, in the shape of humankind, but it was the shape of humankind distorted. Although not particularly tall, not exactly the giants he had envisioned as a child, they were enormously broad and as heavily muscled as an auroch bull. They had hair as animals have fur, dark hair, brown or black, which grew on the faces of the males and on their bodies back and front. They ran with a crouching, loping gait and looked as if they had sufficient strength to run that way forever.

Trotting through the rain shower now, chilled despite his heavy furs and skins, he remembered the day and shuddered at the horror of it all. The scent of the creatures had reached him, so strong and rank he still felt queasy at the memory. He had fled that distant day, and was not ashamed to admit it. He had run and fouled himself in his terror and hidden from the monsters, who had not even seen him.

But he could not hide from destiny.

If the day he remembered had been a horror, the

night he remembered was a nightmare.

It began with a smell, the acrid scent of ogre in the camp. He had decided to track it down. And, though an experienced hunter, he had lost the scent. That was when the nightmare really started.

He had stepped beyond the boundaries of the camp, though not beyond the boundaries of the light cast by the ringfires, and the monster had loomed out of the darkness like a creature from the frozen hells beyond dreamtime.

What a sight it was! From a distance, the ogres had looked frightening and ugly. Now that one was beside him, reaching for him, he realized words like "frightening" and "ugly" had no meaning. The monster was a horror beyond the reach of human minds. Its face was hideous, deformed by a heavy ridge of bone across the brow, which gave it an eternal frown. It had a massive jaw, and teeth so huge, so savage, that the creature could have crunched through bone as easily as a cave bear might break a dried-up twig. Its eyes were wide and brown and full of hate.

While Hiram wondered if he would faint from terror before he could run away, the monster seized him.

Hiram was strong, even by the standards of his tribe. But strong as he was, he was still a babe in arms once the brute gripped him. He struggled, he fought, he struck out, he hit, but nothing made the slightest difference. The creature swung him off the ground as easily as if he weighed no more than a bird. Then there was the ghastly journey to the ogres' cave. Hiram was actually carried most of the way.

He found he could no longer remember that journey very clearly. It had taken him into the dark forest; then he was in a clearing, facing a looming cliff. Then within the cliff itself in a warren of filthy, smelly passageways. And finally he stood inside a massive cavern, surrounded by ogres.

If the creature that had seized him had seemed a nightmare at the time, it was positively handsome compared with the brutes who scratched and grunted, snarled and bickered in that cavern. There was one especially, graying a little, but bigger, stronger, uglier and more bad-tempered than all the rest.

Only the ogres' own fury had saved him on that occasion. They were so naturally bad-tempered and grew so infuriated arguing which should be the one to eat him that they fought among themselves. Hiram, ever fleet of mind as well as foot, had seized the opportunity to flee the cave.

They had followed him, howling like demons,

in a chase through darkened passageways that had been repeated since then a hundred times over in his dreams. He had run until he feared his heart would burst, but he would have pushed himself quite happily beyond the point of death in order to escape.

Escape he had, if only just, although it took the miracle of the Skull of Saber to save him.

The rain stopped, but the memories lingered. He could see the closer edges of the vast dark forest clinging to the northwestern horizon. There, somewhere, was where he had first seen the monsters that haunted his dreams. There they were still, lurking in their caverns or prowling the forest depths, waiting for some unwary human to venture into their domain.

But that unwary human would not be Hiram. Nothing, nothing on earth, would persuade him ever again to enter the dark forest. For nothing, nothing on earth, could ever frighten him as much as those monstrous denizens of the—

His very thought froze in midstream. Locked into his memories, he had topped a rise without attention to the world around him and started down the slope before he realized he had run—not walked but *run*—into the fringes of a mammoth herd.

The great beasts towered around him, their shaggy coats still dripping from the recent rain, living mountains of flesh and bone and muscle, curved tusks soaring, black eyes glinting. These monsters made the ogres of his recent thoughts seem smaller than a Henka tribesman. They were the largest of all living creatures, in accordance with the Mother's promise in the dreamtime. They walked where they willed, fearing neither beast nor man and showing little patience with any creature so foolish as to disturb them.

Hiram stopped, his heart jerked into his mouth. Cautiously, he began to back away, then stole a glance over his shoulder and saw two mammoth from the herd were now actually behind him. He must have run straight past them while still in his reverie.

He turned to his right, but there were mammoth to the right of him. He turned to his left and there were mammoth to the left of him. The herd that stretched before him seemed to cover the whole plain. There were scores of them, hundreds— scores of hundreds. He had never seen a bigger herd. And he was surrounded.

A young bull moved with awakening curiosity. He felt the ground tremble at its approach. Black eyes, small by contrast with that massive body, glared at him through the shaggy curtain of gray-brown wool. Each of its soaring tusks was thicker than his arm.

Careless of the beasts behind, Hiram fell back a trembling step. The young bull's trunk went up at once to trumpet an ear-splitting challenge. Other mammoth suddenly took note of the stranger in their midst. They began to lumber toward him.

11

The Barradik Decision

"So," Greffa murmured as Saft whispered into her ear. She nodded. "Yes," she said. "Ah, yes."

"May I take it," Sambaline put in sarcastically, "that the rest of us will share this news at some time before we have to leave for the Star Jamboree?"

Greffa ignored her, attention firmly fixed on Saft. At first the expression on her oily face was unreadable, but gradually her eyes began to glitter.

The change was not lost on Sambaline. "Come, come," she protested coldly. "Surely we are entitled to hear such *interesting* news."

Orani, a supporter of Sambaline and a blunter, less sophisticated individual altogether, muttered, "Enough's enough, Chief. You can't run the inner council as if we were children. What's happened? We deserve to know."

But even the aggressive tone failed to disturb Greffa. She listened for several minutes more before waving Saft away and turning toward the others. Her face might have been carved from stone. "The news is grave," she said.

They waited, staring at her with expressions of anticipation.

Greffa glanced from one face to the other. She dropped her voice as if imparting a secret. "The Hag is dead."

For an instant there was stunned silence in the yurt. Outside, the commotion continued unabated—indeed, if anything, it had worsened. It was easy to imagine the discreet guards had now abandoned their game and stood shoulder to shoulder at the entrance to the tent lest excitement should lead anyone to attempt disruption of the elders' meeting.

"Dead?" Sambaline echoed. She might have realized shock showed in her voice and face, for she made a visible effort to compose herself.

Hai-line, by contrast, merely shrugged. "She was of an age."

And Orani, who made no secret of her dislike of Crones, said cheerfully, "Even that old lizard could not live forever." She smiled at her colleagues, as if expecting agreement.

Greffa said flatly, "She was murdered."

For a moment silence descended again, then shattered as the group erupted into uproar. Suddenly, everyone was talking at once, shouting in order to be heard. Greffa, staring at the floor, allowed it to continue for a time. Then she raised her head. "Be *quiet*!"

The force of her tone shocked them into silence. Greffa looked from one to the other, for once revealing the raw, ruthless strength that had kept her chief of the most powerful tribe throughout a dozen vain attempts to oust her.

She lowered her voice until it was pitched only just above a whisper, so that they had to strain to hear. The harsh expression softened, although a hard gleam remained in her dark eyes. She allowed herself a half smile. "It is best we keep calm. The implications are momentous."

Saft looked as though she were about to speak, but obviously thought better of it, for she closed her mouth without uttering a sound.

Lob, however, asked quietly, "What happens now?"

Greffa shrugged. "A new Hag will be chosen."

"When?"

"Soon. She must be in place before the Star Jamboree. We can assume the Crones will meet at once, when they receive the news."

Frowning, Hai-line said, "I don't suppose there is any chance that our Crone will be Hag?" The elevation of the Barradik Crone to Hag would strengthen Barradik power immeasurably.

But Greffa was shaking her head. "I think we all know who the next Hag will be. There is one among the Crones whose abilities outstrip all others."

Orani turned her head and actually spat on the ground. "The Shingu Crone!" she muttered, both disgust and fear present in her voice. In the matter of the totem, the Shingu Crone was the only reason why the Barradik had not already raided that upstart little tribe and ground their stupid lion skull to dust.

Surprisingly, Greffa said, "It may be no bad thing if she is chosen."

They waited for her to explain, but she elected to wait until one of them spoke. Eventually Orani asked, "What do you mean?"

"If the *Shingu* Crone becomes Hag, she can scarcely select the *Shingu* totem as Star Totem."

There was silence as they took this in. Then it was Sambaline who whispered, "By the Goddess, you are *right*! The tribes would never stand for it."

Greffa smiled. "More important, the Shingu Crone must know this. She is nothing if not cunning."

"Just a minute," Tooma put in. "The Hag is supposed to stand outside tribal loyalties."

"This is politics," Greffa said, "not principles. Of course the Hag is supposed to stand outside tribal loyalties. But more important, the Hag has to be *seen* to stand outside tribal loyalties. Especially a new Hag. If the Shingu Crone becomes Hag and chooses the Shingu totem, there will be talk. They will say she picked it because it was Shingu, not because it was worthy. Even a Hag cannot survive if a majority of the tribes turn against her. The Shingu Crone knows that. She is an ambitious woman. She has honed her skills and walked dark passageways for years now, preparing to become the Hag. She will not jeopardize so hard-won a position for the sake of an old bone."

"Especially," Sambaline said perceptively, "since the Shingu must benefit in other ways from their Crone becoming Hag."

"Precisely," Greffa said. "Chief Renka wants this so-called Skull of Saber to be the new Star Totem because it will bring wealth and power to her tribe. But wealth and power will accrue to her tribe in any case when the Shingu Crone becomes the Hag. Not so quickly, to be sure, and not so much. But we all know it is better to eat the deer we have caught than to release it while we go chasing after others in the herd." She shifted her position and smiled without a hint of warmth. "No, the Shingu will forget their stupid skull and enjoy all that which must derive from the elevation of their Crone, leaving us to hold Star Totem with our Giant's Thighbone as we have done for generations."

"Assuming," said Lob slyly, "that the new Hag picks the thighbone." Although Sambaline was Greffa's most dangerous opponent within the tribe, Lob was the one who took least care to hide her loathing of the leader.

"What other totem matches the Giant's Thighbone for magic?"

"I don't know," Lob admitted. "But then I don't have to. It's the Hag who makes the choice, and the new Hag may decide there is something better."

Greffa refused to be drawn. Still in the same soft tone she said, "Our only danger is the Skull of Saber."

"You have just finished telling us it is no danger," Sambaline said.

Greffa smiled at her as spiders, if they smiled,

102

might smile at flies. "No danger for the Jamboree. No danger for the present. But I must think beyond the present. And I do think beyond the present. That is why I am chief and you, Sambaline, are not."

Sambaline flushed but said nothing. Orani, however, muttered, "What are you talking about, Greffa?"

"I am talking about the Shingu find!" Greffa snapped. "I am talking about this thing they call the Skull of Saber. The old Hag's death may have saved us immediate embarrassment, but the skull remains. Whatever we may say in public, let us not pretend among ourselves. Everything I have heard—and Chief Renka's attitude—convinces me this is a powerful totem indeed. The new Hag may not feel she can select it for the next Jamboree, but the one after that . . ."

"Is ten years away," Sambaline interjected smoothly.

Greffa rounded on her. "And in the meantime? Are you such a fool, woman, that you cannot imagine what will happen in the meantime? This Shingu totem will still be entered at the Jamboree. The Hag may not select it, but it will be seen. It will be talked about. The tribes will see it and they will be impressed. Oh yes, they will be impressed.

Even if it truly contains less magic than the Giant's Thighbone, it is a new totem, and the tribes will always look to something new."

"And it might contain more magic," Hai-line said.

Tooma started to protest, but Greffa talked her down. "Hai-line is right. Listen, all of you—Hai-line is right. And I say that as chieftain of the Barradik. The Shingu may have found a totem that is actually more powerful than our own. They certainly think they have."

Greffa remained silent for a moment, then snapped forward, her eyes abruptly open. "After," she said, "there will be those who will say the skull should have been chosen. There will be those who will say it was not chosen only because the new Hag is Shingu. There will be those who will gravitate toward it and seek to benefit from its magic, whether it was made Star Totem or not. There will be many such, from many tribes. And every one who turns toward the Shingu skull is one less to pay tribute to the Giant's Thighbone. Can you see what this means?"

"Certainly," said Lob. "It means you lose some of your power."

"It means the entire Barradik nation loses

power!'' Greffa spat. "A loss of power for all of us!"

Sambaline, who saw the force of the argument, said only, "What can we do?" There was no edge to her tone. She had obviously decided to make peace with Greffa—at least until the present difficulties were resolved.

Greffa felt the change of atmosphere at once and smiled inwardly. But she allowed nothing to show on her face as she said, "I have not yet told you everything. There are certain developments that present us with a unique opportunity to deal effectively with this situation."

"And those are?"

Greffa glanced across at Saft, who had remained uncharacteristically silent for a long time now. She looked back at the others, her gaze lingering a little on each face. "The Shingu skull was discovered by a child, an orphan by the name of Shiva. This happened two years ago. It was an accident—there is nothing unusual about the child. She was being chased by some beast and happened upon a disused lair in which she found the totem. That is the truth of it." She took a deep breath. "But the Shingu, of course, tell it differently. They say the child, this Shiva, was guided by the Mother Goddess. They claim this child has miraculous powers—she can walk safely among the great cats and converse with monsters and so on. All nonsense, of course, but that is hardly the point. The point is the Shingu have already made many claims that this child Shiva is important. Doubtless they would have made these claims at the Jamboree."

Sambaline, who missed little, said, "*Would have* made these claims at the Jamboree, Chief Greffa? Is there doubt that they will now do so?"

Greffa nodded. It was a pity Sambaline opposed her. The woman had a mind as sharp as any Crone. What an ally she would make if they could only bury their old differences. "I told you the Hag was murdered. I did not tell you a Shingu stands accused of that murder. I did not tell you that Shingu is the child Shiva, the same girl who found the totem skull."

They stared at her.

Saft grinned. "And we have her!"

"Weaver has brought her here," Greffa said. "I shall ensure she is well rewarded for her foresight." Her eyes flickered across their faces. "If the girl Shiva is put on trial and found guilty, it will totally discredit the entire Shingu nation. She who found the skull has blood on her hands—and the blood of a Hag. There is not a tribe in the land who would bow to the Saber totem once that became known."

"So," asked Sambaline, "what do you propose we do?"

Greffa stood. "I propose we convene a court. I propose we hold a public trial. I propose we try this Shingu orphan Shiva." She strode toward the entrance of the yurt, turning as she reached it. "I propose," she added softly, "that we find her guilty and have her quickly put to death."

12

The Magic Steed

Renka crouched, ready to flee. The Crone had placed one thin, liver-spotted hand on the mare's neck and the animal had not even twitched; it had turned its head and actually nuzzled the witch. This was sorcery of a high and terrifying order.

"Is she ill?" Renka whispered, knowing full well the mare was not ill.

"Not ill," said the Crone as if reflecting her thought. She turned to the sturdy pony and said with every indication of affection, "You're not ill, are you, old girl?"

Renka shuddered. "You have bewitched her?"

"In a way," agreed the Crone. She patted the creature's neck and still it did not shy away.

"Can she talk?" asked Renka.

The Crone glanced at her in surprise. "Talk?"

"You speak to her, Sister. I was wondering if she could talk back."

For a long moment the Crone stared at her, then, for the first time in living memory, her face broke into a smile. But it was a slow, bitter smile. "I talk to her, Leader, because I am old and I am lonely and people fear me. Who else should I talk to but a horse?" She shook her head. "She cannot talk back."

Nervously bewildered, Renka asked cautiously, "But she understands you?"

The Crone nodded gravely. "Oh yes. Oh yes, she understands me. Sometimes far too well."

Renka moved forward slowly, as a hunter might. What manner of magic was this that held a wild animal so still? She glanced at the Crone with renewed admiration and a growing excitement. With such magic, the tribe need never hunger again. She imagined herds of deer, of auroch cattle, still and trusting when the hunters came to kill them. In fact, there would be no need for hunter's skills— a child could slaughter them in this state.

And there would be no need to fear the largest lion, the fiercest bear. With this magic, they would be stilled in their tracks, turned aside with a glance. They could be talked to and they would understand. Renka thought of herself approaching a great cat, poised on the carcass of its prey. *Go away cat and leave me the deer*, she would say to it. And the cat, who understood, would obey.

"When are you going to eat her?" Renka asked.

"Eat her?" The Crone's features hardened, like stone.

Confused, Renka asked, "Is this not why you have bewitched her, Sister?"

The Crone looked at her, face softening like the features of an adult speaking to a foolish child. "No, Renka, I have not bewitched her to eat her. Perhaps it is even wrong to say I have bewitched her at all. Rather I have *befriended* her."

Renka stared from Crone to mare, saying nothing. How was it possible to befriend a wild animal, especially one as fleet as a pony?

"There are certain animals that will accept a woman's friendship," said the Crone. Absently, she stroked the mare's neck. "The horse is one of them. Few know this, even among the Crones. It requires a gentle touch and patience—much patience. But once the animal is befriended, it will accept all humankind, not simply her who taught it trust."

"If you do not wish to eat her, Sister, then why . . . ?"

"Renka," said the Crone, not unkindly, "your head is so full of marvels that you have forgotten our dilemma. Shiva is taken by the Barradik. They seek her death—of that I am certain. I believe you can save her, but as you have said, the camp of the Barradik is close on a day's march distant. Even should you run your heart out, you might not reach her in time. That is why I decided you must meet my friend the mare. She will carry you to Shiva."

Renka, who had been creeping cautiously toward the pony, froze into stunned immobility. Her gaze flickered from the Crone to the animal and back. She raised a hand in the manner of one warding off a blow, then dropped it again. Eventually she said, "*Carry* me?"

The Crone nodded.

"Upon her back?"

"Yes."

"To the encampment of the Barradik?"

"Yes."

Renka fell silent, an expression close to panic on her face. The Crone waited calmly. The pony, almost incredibly, lowered her head to graze.

Questions tumbled through Renka's mind like a landslide, jostling for position and expression. But in the end she asked only, "How will she find her way?"

And the Crone said only, "You will guide her."

For a long moment nothing happened. The tumbling questions still in Renka's mind grew so urgent, she could voice none of them. This time it was the Crone who broke the silence. "Climb upon her back, Renka."

Renka only stared at her.

The Crone said flatly, "Climb upon her back."

"She will bite me," Renka said.

"She will not bite you," the Crone said. "She is my friend, thus she is your friend. Climb upon her back."

"She will kick me."

"She will not kick you. Climb upon her back."

"She will throw me off, Sister."

"She will not throw you off," the Crone said patiently.

"She will carry me to the herd of wild horses and the herd will kill me!" Renka looked around her wildly. Only the disciplines of a lifetime prevented her from running from this magic.

"She will take you only where you wish to go." The Crone moved so that she stood close to Renka and actually placed one hand gently on her arm. Renka shivered. The Crone said quietly, "I smell your fear, Renka. Yet why do you fear? Have I ever wished you harm?"

Dumbly, Renka shook her head. For the first time in a hard life, she felt close to tears.

"Watch!" instructed the Crone. She turned, ran three short steps and, with astonishing agility for one so old, vaulted astride the back of the mare. The pony looked up, startled, and backed a few short steps, but otherwise made no attempt to harm her rider. "See?" called the Crone. "She accepts me." She reached down and gripped the pony's mane, then whispered something in one twitching ear. At once the mare set off around the glade, the old witch on her back.

The circuit completed, the Crone drew up beside Renka. "See?" she said again. "She takes me where I wish to go." She slid from the back of the animal, which, relieved of its burden, commenced to graze again as if nothing unusual had happened. "Then she walked," said the Crone. "But on open ground and especially on the plain, she will run. She will run like the wind and carry you to the camp of the Barradik!"

"I will fall off, Sister!" Renka howled.

But the Crone's eyes glittered with excitement. "You must cling on. You hold on with your legs, your thighs, and when she runs you may wrap your arms around her neck. It is not so difficult."

"Not so difficult . . ." Renka echoed. She was staring at the pony, which stood as high as her shoulder.

"Of course," said the Crone, "if your arms are around her neck, you cannot guide her. So when you wish to guide her, you must hold on with your legs alone."

"I will *die!*" Renka exclaimed. It had never before occurred to her to disobey the Crone, but there was conflict in her soul that brought her close to defiance now.

"Did I die?"

"You are Crone!" Renka blurted, close to shouting.

"It was friendship that kept me on the mare, not magic," the Crone insisted irritably. She glared. "Climb on her back!"

"Sister, do not make me—"

"Climb," hissed the Crone, "upon her back."

Miserably, reluctantly, as if she had become a little girl again, Renka moved toward the mare. It looked up at her approach, but otherwise did not move. She reached the beast, standing so close that its scent filled her nostrils to the exclusion of all else. The mare ignored her, bent again to graze.

"Take hold of her mane," the Crone commanded.

"She will kick me. She will bite me," Renka muttered, reaching all the same for the shaggy

114

mane. The mare continued grazing as before and neither kicked nor bit.

"Vault upon her back."

Renka closed her eyes and offered up a rare prayer to the Mother. In a lifetime marked by danger, she had never felt so frightened, not even when she had faced the ogre horde. She tightened her grip on the mane, opened her eyes and jumped.

She was astride the mare, flattened on the sturdy back, her face pressed against the pony's neck. She threw her arms around and clung, firmly, expecting the beast to panic and flee, taking her she knew not where.

But the pony did not panic, only danced a little back and forth and whinnied lightly. Renka could feel the warmth of the sturdy beast, the play of powerful muscles beneath the shaggy pelt. She was aware—desperately aware—of every tiny movement, but the pony did not buck or rear or try to throw her as it might have done had some predator leaped upon its back. Nor did it run away.

Eventually, heart beating fiercely, Renka eased her panic-powerful grip upon the creature's neck and slowly sat upright. The Crone was watching her approvingly. The sacred grove had taken on a new perspective, viewed now from a giant's height.

A small bubble of excitement tightened Renka's stomach. She smiled, uncertainly at first, then with increasing confidence.

"Nudge her with your knees," the Crone instructed. "Ask her to walk."

"Walk, horse," Renka said, remembering this animal understood human speech. The mare ambled off, completing the circuit of the grove without further instruction. Renka watched the trees move past with awe and wonder. The pony carried her! She felt a surge of joy and power. The Crone had given her a magic steed, and seated on its sturdy back, she could fly across the plains to rescue Shiva.

At that moment, Renka felt she could reach out her arms and crush the entire Barradik tribe.

13
The Trial

"Death!" murmured Lob.

There was a vast open space in the center of the Barradik encampment, cleared of stones and shrub and grass and already beaten flat by many feet. The rows of brown-black yurts marched out from it like the deformed trees of some forest, stretching into the plain on three sides, toward the real forest on the fourth. It was here that they had dragged Shiva for her trial.

They had never been kind to her, not from the first moment of their meeting at the water hole. But now they were positively brutal. The flat-faced man with the portion missing from his ear struck her twice across the face as an encouragement to walk faster. Another of the men gripped her arm with such force that bruises appeared beneath his fingers. The woman Weaver had been replaced by someone Shiva did not know, a tall, muscular creature with unkempt hair, and this woman shouted orders at Shiva in so thick an accent that Shiva could not understand them. Not understanding, she could not obey. Not obeying, she was struck by the woman about the head until her ears rang.

"Show no weakness," warned the imaginary figure of her mother, who had appeared to comfort her when she had first been marched into this threatening camp.

But Shiva did not need the warning. She neither protested nor cried out nor made any sound. No tears sprang to her eyes. She took the pain as it came and walked through the pain in her mind so that it stood behind her. After each beating, her body stung and ached, but she separated herself from the pain and watched it as if it belonged to another. She stared blankly at her captors. She would show no weakness.

"Death." Sambaline nodded.

As they convened the trial, the Barradik Crone appeared in order to make magic. She was not as old as the Crone of Shiva's tribe, nor as tall. In build, she reminded Shiva a little of her tribal chieftain Renka: the same square shoulders, the same muscular legs. But there the resemblance ended.

118

Her face was round like the face of the moon and cratered with the remnants of some childhood pox. She had very tiny blue-gray eyes, without warmth. She wore the working clothes of so many Crones, the pelt of a black cave bear. She carried fire—a small, smoldering fire streaming smoke—in a portion of a human skull.

The Crone set the smoking skull upon the ground. She drew a package of mottled doeskin from somewhere inside her furs and set it beside the skull before beginning to unwrap it. But she did not unwrap the pack completely. Instead she thrust in her hand with a motion that was almost angry. She pulled out a fist of gray-white dust, called once and blew it to the north, called twice and blew it to the east, called thrice and blew it to the south, called four times and blew it to the west.

Shiva watched the Barradik Crone's performance of weather magic impassively. She found the Barradik Crone an unimpressive figure, more like an elderly warrior than a Crone. Certainly no sense of power clung to her as it clung to the Shingu Crone. Perhaps—

But before she could finish the thought, one of the men was dragging her forward, shaking her as a jackal shakes its prey. When he ceased and she recovered her senses, she could see Barradik tribes-

119

people, men and women both, streaming between the yurts to join the crowd already in the central square. There was excitement on their faces, as if they were attending one of the great gatherings in celebration of the Mother.

There were seven elders present, squatting together in the northern quadrant of the clearing. Shiva knew they were elders because they had stained their faces purple with the juice of a plant. Someone, long ago, had told her the elders of the great Barradik tribe had purple faces. It had seemed silly to her then, so silly she had not really believed it. Yet there they were, seven women with bright-purple faces set above their skins and furs. It no longer looked silly to Shiva. It looked frightening.

She would show no fear. Fear was weakness and she was determined she would show no weakness.

''*Death!*'' cackled the scar-faced Saft. She seemed to find something amusing about the word.

It had taken Shiva a little while to realize what was happening, but the signs eventually became unmistakable. A trial had been convened. She did not need to be told who was being tried.

And yet she could not quite believe it was really happening. Not to her. There had been no warnings, no ill omens. A day like any other day when she had gone to the water hole to wash. And now she was in this strange place, surrounded by these strange people, facing these strange elders with their purple faces, accused of murdering the Crone of Crones.

How could they think it? How could they possibly imagine she would have harmed that tiny, frail old woman in any way, let alone *kill* her? It was unthinkable. Yet here she was, facing the elders of the Barradik.

She tried not to think what they would do to her if they believed her to be guilty of this crime, but her mind refused to obey the urgings of her will and thought about it all the same. The universal penalty for murder—murder of any sort— was death. But she stood accused of a very special, very hideous murder. She stood accused of the murder of the Hag, the Crone of Crones. What penalty could match such a crime?

The Barradik had already shown themselves cruel, a tribe of careless violence, quite unlike her native Shingu. Surely such a tribe would attempt to match the penalty to the crime, would attempt to make her death as hideous as the murder she was supposed to have committed.

"Death," growled Tooma, her eyes cast down upon the ground.

Shiva stared inward and contemplated her fate.

She formed the pictures in her mind. She saw herself killed slowly, painfully, at the hands of these Barradik barbarians; and yet she did not cry out, either in pain or in fear. It was important not to show weakness.

She stood, still as a stone, face expressionless. She would not show weakness.

The sky clouded and it began to rain lightly. So much for the power of the Barradik Crone.

"Death!" Hai-line shrugged, face impassive, as if she were instructing her hunters to slaughter an auroch calf.

In the Shingu tribe, no trial would be held without the Crone. It was she who decided on innocence or guilt (although the sentence was decided by the elder council).

"Death!" growled Orani, almost angrily.

But the Barradik Crone played no part in Shiva's trial beyond her single act of futile weather magic. The elders, with their purple faces gleaming in the rain, listened to the stories of Weaver and her men—who told them fairly enough, even the flat-faced man with the injured ear. Then they looked at Shiva's bone club, which had been taken from her, and examined the brown stains on the head. Then they examined the frail, pathetic body of the Hag, its face made ghastly by the shattered skull.

The rain turned briefly to drizzle, then stopped.

Greffa pushed herself to her feet, leaning on the arm of a warrior guard, although she was by no means an old woman. She scarcely glanced at Shiva, but instead allowed her eyes to sweep across the crowd. A sudden silence descended. The cloud cover lightened, but did not break, casting a chill, gray light across the scene.

"You have heard the verdict of the elders," Greffa said, her voice powerful, pitched to carry. "The Shingu girl Shiva stands condemned for murder of the Hag." She glanced toward the guards, closed her eyes briefly and added more softly, "Take her to a high place and stone her to death."

"No!" Shiva screamed in sudden terror. "No! No!"

But the scream was only in her mind. Her face revealed nothing of the inner turmoil. *She would show no weakness.*

14
Shiva Found

Hiram ran.

It was an instinctive, mindless act, driven by the explosive power of a hunter's muscles. He ran first toward an old bull, which watched his approach curiously, then swerved so that he dashed between two towering cows.

Legs pumping with the fury of his panic, he leaped a small rock, turned sharply from his course in order to avoid three more of the huge beasts and actually hurtled underneath the legs of another. The mammoth trumpeted in surprise and swung its head to stare after him. Weaving and ducking, he was suddenly clear of the herd. There was open plain before him. If he could only, somehow, outrun them.

As a hunter, Hiram was accustomed to covering

large distances in search of game. But these were covered in the hunter's trot, a deliberate, loping gait more suited to endurance than speed. Now he was running flat out, heart pounding, muscles straining, running like the wind. As yet he felt no strain, but how long could he keep this up? He had never thought of mammoth as particularly speedy beasts, but they were truly gigantic, with each stride covering much ground.

And over short distances, he suddenly remembered, they could travel as fast as a charging rhino. Still running flat out, he glanced over his shoulder. The herd was grazing peacefully.

Hiram slowed, then stopped. Cautiously he turned. He had been right. The herd really was grazing peacefully. Not one single mammoth had started after him. He was too small, too insignificant to provoke more than token curiosity in the huge beasts. For a moment he found it upsetting, then realized how lucky he was. If even one of the mammoths had charged, he would be flat as a cowpat now.

He squatted, staring toward the herd. They were magnificent animals, the very largest of all the Mother's creatures, more powerful than the lion and the bear. And yet they ate no meat. He watched them tugging up the long grass, stripping the bushes and the small clumps of low-growing trees. Perhaps he had panicked too quickly. Perhaps he might have walked calmly through the middle of the herd.

All the same, the trail he had been following led directly through the herd. He had not been so lost to his surroundings as to wander from the trail. It was not good news. The herd was huge, strung out across the plain. He would have to detour for miles to skirt its edge. But to detour meant to lose the trail. Would he be able to pick it up again?

Hiram shrugged. He had long since learned it was futile to worry over that which could not be avoided. All he could do was skirt the herd and hope he would get lucky when he reached the other side. He stood and trotted off, watching the mammoths warily out of the corner of his eye. But though he was only a few hundred paces away, none paid him any heed. And after a time he came to realize there was an unexpected benefit to his position. Paying full attention now, he smelled no cat or bear, saw no bison or auroch bull. Everything kept clear of the herd—*everything*. The great beasts were so powerful in themselves that the area around the herd must be the safest earth in the world. Hiram felt at once frightened and comforted. It was a curious combination.

Skirting the herd took him far longer than he had anticipated. It seemed to stretch forever. But eventually he was able to turn north again, then, perhaps two hours later, swing around in a wide circle in the hope that he could once again pick up the trail.

He could not pick up the trail.

The mammoth herd was constantly shifting. Although it was still cold, the sun was now high in the sky and the ground no longer frozen. Many areas where the herd had passed were muddy, churned and broken. The huge feet of the beasts had obliterated every sign other than their own.

With steadily mounting panic, Hiram ranged farther and farther in his attempt to find some indication of where the Barradik were headed. Where had they taken Shiva? *Why* had they taken Shiva? The questions hammered at his mind like drumbeats. And with the first two came a third: What did the Barradik plan to do with Shiva?

He had to find her, find the camp, before it was too late. Too late for what? He did not know. But he feared. How he feared!

Half weeping with frustration, he examined the ground for a sign and once again found nothing.

He was getting nowhere. It occurred to him his only hope was an overview. If he climbed a tree or found high ground, he might be able to see far enough to get some indication of where Shiva had been taken by her captors. Hard on the thought, he clambered up a rocky escarpment, looked—and caught his breath.

The black, conical tents of the Barradik marched across the far horizon like warriors ranged ready for war. And beyond them the sinister outlines of the dark forest, the same dark forest where Hiram had once faced those most hideous of monsters, the ogres hungering for human brains. He shivered involuntarily. How could any tribe, however powerful, select a campsite so close to the ogres' lair?

But the thought was swallowed by an immediate realization. He had found the Barradik camp! By accident or destiny, he had found the Barradik! Was Shiva somewhere there among the yurts? It did not matter, for if she was not among the yurts, she surely would be soon. The party of Barradik who took her at the water hole could only be headed here.

What to do? Hiram squatted down, his back against a rock, keen eyes raking the distant encampment, considering his position.

It was likely, he thought, that Shiva was already there, somewhere in that giant camp. The Barradik party that had taken her at the water hole had had a considerable head start on him—just how considerable he could only guess. And they had not had to skirt the mammoth herd as he had. Traveling directly to their camp, they must have arrived long ago, hours ago. Thus Shiva was held there, ahead, among the yurts.

What to do? Quite suddenly, Hiram found himself bitterly regretting the impetuous decision to follow the trail alone. How could he expect to rescue Shiva from among so many? When he had found evidence of Shiva taken, he should have run directly to the tribe and there told Renka or whatever elder he could find. The elders would have raised a rescue party. It might not have arrived so quickly, but—

But what? The whole Shingu tribe could not march upon the Barradik. There were too many. No rescue party could free Shiva. If the Barradik had her, they could hold her against attack by any other tribe. So perhaps he had not been so foolish after all.

Was it possible, he wondered, to free Shiva by stealth? First, of course, he would have to find her. But that, the hunter in him knew, was only a question of time and patience. Now that he had found the camp, he must sooner or later find where Shiva was held, provided he could move freely within the camp.

The thought of entering the Barradik encampment frightened him, but he considered it just the same. In so large a tribe, would a stranger be noticed? Most Barradik men put black feathers in their hair and dyed their faces yellow, but not all—surely not all. And besides, what was there to stop him from putting feathers in *his* hair and dying *his* face yellow? He even knew the plant that produced the dye. It was common enough at this season, and a handful of the flowers would be enough to stain his face. And he could find some feathers for his hair.

Apart from that, the Barradik dressed no differently from the Shingu, looked no different from the Shingu. The arms they carried were not those typically carried by a Shingu hunter, but there was so much variety among the Barradik that even this difference might well go unnoticed.

Hiram pushed himself upright, climbed down from the escarpment and went in search of the bush he needed. He proved to be in luck, for only minutes later he caught the flash of yellow that told him he had succeeded.

He gathered the flowers quickly. He hesitated for

a moment, staring at the flowers. He had no idea what the Barradik actually did with them to extract the yellow juice. Eventually he crushed them in his hands and rubbed them vigorously into the skin of his face. Petals dropped like snowflakes onto his furs, and the palms of his hands at least turned yellow. Had his face done the same?

He trotted back the way he had come, looking for the pool of rainwater he had noticed trapped in a hollow in a rock. On the way, he found a gift from the Mother, the half-eaten body of a crow. With a surge of pleasure that almost washed away his fear, he plucked the bird, sticking wing and tail feathers in his hair.

The sun emerged from behind a cloud just as he reached the rock pool. He leaned forward and stared at his reflection. A yellow-faced Barradik stared back at him, the color brilliant in the sunlight. The black feathers were, he thought, very becoming; but apart from that, the difference made by the dye was dramatic. His own mother might have mistaken him for a Barradik—at least at a distance.

When he finished admiring himself, he noticed the yellow stain still clung to his hands and tried to wash it off in the pool. It proved remarkably stubborn, and in the end he could remove it only by scrubbing with earth and gravel. He stood up, adjusted his furs, then trotted off toward the Barradik camp.

He moved, both instinctively and consciously, as a hunter moves, searching out cover, remaining hidden where possible and moving quickly when he was caught in the open. And he stopped well short of the yurts, on a ridge overlooking the western tip of the encampment, a little too near to the edge of the dark forest for his liking, but with enough boulders and rocks to allow him to remain hidden. He would not, he had decided, try to enter the camp just yet. Better to wait for rain or, if absolutely necessary, dusk, when there was less chance of his attracting attention. He slid into shadow between two rocks and waited.

He did not enjoy waiting, since it gave him far too much time to think. Did he really imagine he was going to succeed in this lunatic endeavor? The camp was enormous. Shiva might be confined in any of the yurts. He would have to pass for a Barradik, mingle with Barradik men—and worse still, Barradik women—until he actually found Shiva. Doubtless she would be guarded, so he must make a plan to get past her guards. Then he would have to rescue her and somehow conduct her safely from the camp. After that he would have to get her home to the Shingu camp, quite probably forced to travel in darkness. It was a nightmare to contemplate. Nonetheless, he waited.

As he waited, his hunter's instincts prompted him to study the encampment. It was so totally different from anything in his personal experience that it might have fallen from the dreamtime.

The yurts, he could now see, were constructions of animal skins and animal bones, although without going closer, he had no idea of how they were erected, or what magic was used to prevent their blowing down. Or burning down, come to that, since several seemed to have fires within.

Something tickled his foot, and he glanced down in time to see a snake slide away into a crevice. The markings told him at once it was harmless, but his heart thumped just the same. Then he heard the noise, a swelling hum that grew like the approach of a gigantic swarm of bees. He looked back toward the camp and froze. Barradik men and women were pouring from it like an overflowing river, pushing, jostling and cursing one another in a frenzy of excitement.

At their head, half dragged by two tall warriors, was Shiva.

Hiram flattened himself back, suddenly fearful of being seen, but the crowd was not moving in his direction. Instead they streamed east toward a flat-topped hill. Where were they going? What were they doing?

Shiva seemed pale and drawn, almost ill. Hiram's eyes were keen: He saw at once the bruising on her face and arms and the matting of her hair. She had been beaten by the Barradik—and badly. The realization brought an eruption of fury that almost sent him racing toward this whole foul tribe, shouting his rage. But good sense fought and won the battle, so he held back.

But should he hold back? His rage died and was replaced by hunter's calculation. Should he hold back? The crowd was in a frenzy of excitement. What better time to join it? Who would pay attention to one more yellow face?

The more he thought about it, the more sense it made. Although if he joined the crowd, what did he propose to do then? There was no saving Shiva now, not while she remained the center of attention. The question was, what was being done to her? She had already been badly beaten. What more was planned?

Hiram moved from the cover of the rocks, scarcely aware he had made his decision. The ridge dropped sheer for more than thirty feet, so he could not go directly to the streaming crowd. But he ran quickly in the opposite direction, planning to circle when he reached the lower ground. As he ran, a strange scent reached him, part animal, part something else that he did not recognize. The smell carried no real overtones of danger, no hint of cat or bear, merely a warning that something odd was nearby. As a precaution he drew his club.

Hiram ran from the shelter of the rocks and almost cannoned into the source of the scent. He stopped at once, slack jawed. The raised club slipped from nerveless fingers. Hiram's eyes widened in pure terror.

15

Renka's Ride

It was as a bird flies, as a deer runs. She felt the wind in her face, in her hair. Icy fingers of air slipped between her furs and skins, chilling her. Her back ached and there were bruises on the insides of her thighs, but she did not care. She felt joy such as she had never felt before, not even as a child. The pony carried her!

Renka smiled into the wind. Always she had shied away from magic, for it frightened her greatly. Even the healing arts of the Crone made her irritable and nervous. But *this* magic was a wonder, a miracle. This magic made her want to shout aloud, to scream the news to the land, the sky, the dreamtime itself.

It had all felt so strange at first. The pony would walk daintily from here to there at the command of the Crone. And Renka, on its back, would sway and slip and convince herself she was about to fall off, despite the rigid grip of her knees. But she did not fall off; and eventually, at the urging of the Crone, she relaxed enough to go with the movement.

The Crone told her she could guide the mare by tugging on its mane. As went the head, so went the horse. Pull the head to the right, and the mare went right. Pull the head to the left, and left she went. In the beginning, Renka pulled strongly, almost jerking, but she soon discovered a gentle tug was enough. Later still, she found out something very odd. She could guide the mare without touching her mane at all, just by squeezing with her knees and leaning a little in the direction she wanted to go. It soon became that she seemed only to think of a change in direction for the pony to obey, as if reading her thoughts. This was the strangest thing of all, for it felt as if she and the beast were one, no longer woman and mare, but a curious animal that combined the two.

After walking, she gained sufficient confidence to encourage the pony to run. The movement jarred her spine and left her bottom sore, so she wondered how she could possibly travel any distance in such a manner. But then, quite suddenly, she caught the rhythm and after that sat easy.

The sun had already climbed high in the sky by this point, but the Crone showed no impatience, no concern. All the same, when she was certain Renka could handle the pony, she sent her off quickly enough, directing her first south and west before turning back north so that she could avoid riding through the camp and upsetting the tribe.

At first the going was rough, over stony ground and through shrub. The marvelous creature beneath her was sure-footed enough, but picked its way with care, thus slowly. Still Renka marveled, for already she traveled faster than she would on foot—and without effort.

They followed the course of the river for a time. Renka kept the mare well away from the water, which was running fast enough to make the banks unsafe, but from her new, elevated vantage point she could see the torrent easily through its curtain of trees. The water boiled white with muddy depths beneath and seemed to have burst its banks farther upstream, to judge by the amount of timber swept along.

She felt very alive, as if her senses had been washed in morning dew and sharpened like a piece of flint. She saw everything, heard everything, smelled everything. At one point she even thought she could taste everything: the wind in her face, the river to the west, the vegetation and the foliage. The sensation was beyond anything she had ever experienced. She felt a power in herself she had never known she owned and wondered if this was how the Crone felt when she made her magic. If so, it would explain why Crones so readily endured the hardships of their profession for so little obvious return. To feel like this was to feel equal to the Mother Goddess herself. Renka blushed at the thought, but acknowledged its truth nonetheless.

They followed the river, Renka and her magic steed, until they reached a stand of trees too dense for comfort and turned east, then northeast and finally north. Soon the going became more open and the pony picked up speed.

Earlier, when the Crone had told her she must rescue Shiva, Renka had felt fearful, worried, uncertain. Now these emotions were gone, swept away by the elation of this magic. Of course she would rescue Shiva! Nothing was impossible anymore.

She guided the pony across an area of scree and down a slope into a narrow, shallow valley strewn with rocks and boulders. The mare disliked the place at once—Renka could feel her nervousness—but moved obediently enough at her rider's command.

An errant thought came to Renka. Why not mount the hunt? There were herds of horses so large, they were like grains of sand on a beach. If the Crone worked her magic, why not mount the entire tribe?

The thought almost overwhelmed her. No longer would they need to walk from campsite to campsite—the horses would carry them. If danger threatened and they were required to run, the horses would carry them; and faster and farther than they could ever manage now. They could run from the flood, from the forest fire. They could hunt game and run from danger.

And the horses could carry meat for them. The horses ate grass and so would not eat the meat. But they could carry it. She was not exactly certain how, but she thought that if a deer were slung across her pony's back, she should be able to hold it on. It might be difficult, but it would certainly be less difficult than carrying the deer herself.

The thoughts were beginning to tumble through her mind faster and faster, exciting her greatly. The Shingu, her Shingu, would become the tribe of tribes. What other tribe had such magic? To the Shingu had come the Skull of Saber; and now to the Shingu had come the magic steed. They would not hunger. They could flee from any danger. Their numbers would multiply and they would grow strong, the strongest of all the tribes, stronger even than the Barradik.

And she would be remembered. The songs would sing of Renka, who led the Shingu at the time of the Great Change!

They were nearing the mouth of the valley, where it emerged onto the flatlands. Her pony felt more nervous than ever and moved ahead quickly, without urging, as if anxious to quit the valley.

Perhaps, Renka thought, the mare was sensing some of her excitement. Was it really possible the Shingu could outgrow the Barradik? In her deepest heart, she knew it was. And the magic was already beginning. First the skull, then the steed, and who knew what else the Crone—

The wind changed and she smelled it too—cat! No wonder the pony was nervous. There was a lioness close by.

"Go!" whispered Renka to her steed. The valley narrowed ahead, running between two overhanging rocks before opening into the plain. Despite the

141

rough ground, the pony broke into an immediate canter, heading directly for the opening without guidance.

The lions broke cover at once, not one but a pride of three: two lionesses and, surprisingly, a smallish, heavily maned male. Renka felt the mare surge beneath her with such sudden panic that she almost tumbled off. But she threw her arms around the pony's neck and clung as the canter changed into a wild, uncaring gallop. They passed between the rocks through the narrow neck of the valley and onto the open plain, but the lions were still after them.

Renka knew how quickly a hunting lioness could travel when she charged. Over a short distance she could outrun anything the Goddess ever made. But only over a short distance. Lions had no staying power. They might stalk a herd or lie in ambush, but if that one burst of speed did not take them to their prey, the chances were good that the prey would escape. The Mother alone knew how long this pride had been stalking Renka and her pony. Lions avoided humankind, but horse meat was among their favorite foods. Doubtless they had caught the scent of the mare and ignored the strange figure on her back.

It occurred to Renka she had been lucky with

the wind change. Lions were skilled hunters, especially when they hunted as a pride. They would stalk and circle with great patience, seeking always to trap their selected prey. The narrow valley had been perfect for such a trap. Had even one of the three managed to get ahead, the mouth of the valley would have been effectively sealed. The male would likely have been chosen for this job, appearing maned and magnificent to drive the pony back to where the lionesses waited. It would be the lionesses who made the actual kill. Male lions were lazy, and most preferred not to hunt at all, let alone take down a running prey.

But they were clear of the valley, clear of the trap. With her magic steed, Renka could easily outrun the pride in the open. And how the pony could run! It was sweating with fear and straining across the plain far faster than it had ever run before. Despite her own fear Renka found the experience exhilarating. She glanced back, fully expecting to see the lions dropping behind. But only the male was losing ground. Both lionesses were running steadily, no more than twenty paces away.

"Go!" Renka screamed to encourage her mount. And as if she knew there was a chance her prey might get away, the leading lioness charged.

Even Renka, who had seen lions hunt before,

could scarcely believe the speed. One moment she was loping along, scarcely keeping pace with the mare. The next she was closing the gap at an alarming rate.

Instinctively, the pony responded, she was no longer under Renka's control, but a wild thing running for her life. Renka would not have believed she could possibly travel any faster, but she did, hooves drumming like distant thunder and the landscape turning to a blur.

Yet the charging lioness was gaining. The male had dropped well back now, tired or bored with the whole thing. The second lioness held to a steady speed, muscles rippling beneath her tawny hide as if she were loping through some easy game of chase-and-catch with her cubs. But the leading lioness was gaining like an avalanche. The twenty paces shrank almost instantly to ten, and then to five.

The pony swerved, and Renka, caught entirely unawares, slipped from its back. Only her fastest, most unthinking reflexes stopped her from falling off completely. As it was, she clung to the pony's side, arms flung around its neck, the ground so close now she could have reached out easily to touch it.

She was sliding, sliding . . . In a moment she

would be hanging beneath the pony. In a moment more, she would have fallen off to be smashed on the ground, pounded by the hooves or seized and torn to pieces by the approaching cats.

With a near super-human effort, Renka began to pull herself slowly upright. She had almost succeeded when the pony swerved again, causing her to slip back down. In an instant of nightmare, she saw the lioness by her side, so close she could actually hear the cat's breathing. Then the pony swerved yet again and the cat disappeared from view.

Heart pounding, Renka jerked herself so savagely that she found herself flattened across the pony's jolting back, her face pressed against the shaggy hide, now slick with sweat. She heard the coughing roar of a lion, but it was the male of the pride, now far behind. Clinging desperately with her knees and holding the mare's mane with both hands, Renka pushed herself upright. The mare was twisting and weaving now like one possessed by ancestral spirits. Renka looked to the right, but could see no lioness; she twisted, but could not see the cat behind. She was turning to her left when the lioness jumped.

Had the pony remained running as she had done, the cat would have been on her back, on Renka too, dragging them both down. But a loose stone beneath the mare's foot caused her to stumble, and in stumbling, a sturdy survival instinct persuaded her to swerve again; and in neither movement did she lose speed.

The cat reared in the air on Renka's left. Renka could actually see her underbelly, the rows of nipples with which she fed her cubs, the lighter-colored fur that half concealed them. There was an impression of raking claws, a furiously twisting body, the broad beautiful cat head. Then the lioness dropped back to the ground, and dropped back from the chase.

The pony had outrun them! Renka could scarcely believe it, yet when she twisted around, all three lions were dropping farther and farther behind; and as she watched, all three, as if by some secret signal, lost interest in the chase, slowed to a stop, stared briefly at her, then turned to stroll toward the valley.

The mare too sensed that the worst of it was over and slowed. Renka felt such a surge of relief that she began to laugh. "We did it, girl!" she shouted to the pony. "We did it! We did it!" The laughter would not stop, although it was now mixed with tears as she patted the pony's neck. "We did it, didn't we? We did it!" Then the pain hit her.

She felt as if her leg had suddenly caught fire. She glanced down and to her utter amazement found her clothing ripped and a bloody slash wound in her thigh. Blood too from her side, above the hip, although this wound was not painful at all. She was bleeding profusely, saturating her furs and the pony's shaggy pelt. The lioness had raked her and she had not even noticed.

What now? Such a wound was death unless she could get quickly to a Crone. Or at least stop the bleeding. She reached down and pinched the edges of her leg wound together, but the blood flowed, hot and slick, around her fingers. The pain grew and the wound in her side began to throb. What to do?

"Hold up," Renka ordered, using the words the Crone had taught her to make the pony stop. But the pony, still frightened by the lions, would not stop. It was no longer in panic flight, but it galloped steadily on, obviously intent on putting as much distance between them and the pride as possible.

What to do? The pain was swelling by the second now, and she felt weakened by the loss of blood. Soon a great darkness would reach out to engulf her, and then the Mother would stretch her arms out from the dreamtime to claim her spirit.

A red haze danced before her eyes. She could

no longer see where they were going. She clung to the pony's back, knees clamped, fingers locked into the shaggy pelt with a final strength born of desperation. Her mind slipped away from her, like one in a fever.

The pony slowed, but did not stop. Renka half turned and voided her stomach onto the ground in one retching, swelling moment. She felt a little better for the action, but weak and very tired. The pain was red and hot and broke over her in waves. Perhaps she should try to sleep. She was suddenly so very, very tired, and sleep would let her escape from the pain.

She could not sleep. She did not think she slept. Perhaps she dozed. The movement of the pony was strangely comforting.

Renka lost all experience of time. There was the motion of the pony and the pain and the weakness. Sometimes she opened her eyes to the red haze, sometimes to a landscape she could no longer recognize. She wondered where the mare was taking her. It was a magic steed, so it must be taking her somewhere. Perhaps it was taking her to its herd, where the Crone of the horses would heal her wounds.

Suddenly, Renka jerked upright, weak, but wide awake. The pony had stopped. She slid in a heap from her mount, crumpled to the ground. For a moment she lay there, too exhausted to move, then slowly, painfully, she rolled on her back and opened her eyes. A Barradik warrior stood over her, club raised.

16

The Execution

She would show . . . no . . . *weakness*!

Shiva gritted her teeth and held back the sounds of her pain and terror. They were going to kill her. These filthy, painted Barradik were going to stone her to death!

She was dragged stumbling from the place of the trial, marched between two yellow-faced men along the endless rows of yurts. And as they marched, the Barradik tribe, the *entire* Barradik tribe, it seemed, swarmed around her like demented ants.

So many Barradik; and in crowds, the Barradik were worse, much worse, than any Barradik alone. The stench of unwashed bodies hung heavily in the air, overlaid by a scent of excitement expressed from a thousand glands. There was anger on their faces, and hatred. She had never seen such a manifestation of hatred, let alone experienced it directed against herself.

Anger and hatred—yet behind both was a keen enjoyment. They were going to stone her to death and they were going to love every moment of it.

The noise dinned in on her like a physical thing: a hum, like a swarm of giant bees, overlaid with shouts, jeers, catcalls. One man, thin and wrinkled as the Shingu Crone, but nearly toothless and with shifty eyes, actually danced before her, grimacing, giggling, making obscene gestures until one of her guards pushed him rudely out of the way. He danced into the crowd calling cheerfully, "You'll soon be put to death, Shingu!"

Why? Why did they hate her so much? Because they thought she had killed the Hag? Yet most of these people could never have seen the Hag, never have known her. Even if they thought her guilty of the crime, it did not explain the *personal* nature of their reaction.

"Hurry it up!" one of the guards commanded, jerking her arm so violently that she fell down on both knees. One caught on a jagged edge of stone, sending pain shooting—*I will show no weakness.*—

into the bone and causing a sudden welling of blood. Someone in the crowd laughed. The guard jerked her to her feet again.

How would they do it? She had never seen a stoning. The Shingu had no such penalty, no matter how serious the crime. She tried to imagine what it would be like. At first fear gripped her so tightly that nothing came, then pictures began to form in her mind. She would be taken to a high place, as Chief Greffa had ordered, a high, stony hill. There they would surround her. It would become quiet, tense with expectation. Then one would bend to pick up a stone. She thought it might be the old toothless man who had mocked her with his dance or Greffa herself, who had ordered her death. The stone would be thrown, then another and another. They would bury her beneath a heap of stones.

Was there any way she could escape?

A series of pictures presented themselves before her inner eye. She stood by a raging river, far too dangerous to swim. Then behind her appeared a cave lion, and she dived into the river and swam. Because the river was the lesser danger. She stood on the edge of a cliff, knowing she would die if she jumped. Then a charging rhino appeared (like the rhino that had charged her on the day she had found the skull) and she jumped over the cliff. Because the cliff was the lesser danger.

She cut the pictures short. Their message was clear enough. Certain escapes would never be attempted unless the alternative was certain death. Certain death by stoning faced her. What escape, however hazardous, was possible?

The guards held her firmly by the arms, their fingers digging deeply, painfully into her skin. They were grown men, burly, far stronger than she. But they would not hold her forever. When the moment came for her to be stoned, they must release her. She would be surrounded, but what if she ran at the crowd? They would not expect such a move. The chances were slim that she would break through, but she might. And if she did, there was one place she might hide, a place so dangerous in the eyes of humankind that none would follow her.

It was the torrent and the cliff, the lesser of two dangers. If she could somehow break through the circling crowd, she would run to the dark forest.

Shiva tripped and fell again. At once both guards fell to punching and kicking her until she dragged—*I will show no weakness!*—herself to her feet again. Her stomach and sides felt bruised and sore, and a sharp pain jabbed her each time she breathed, as if the beating had cracked a rib. She felt the salty taste of blood in her mouth. Nonetheless, she held her head high and walked on, showing nothing. The crowd, excited by the beating, howled like a pack of wolves.

Could she break through? None would dare follow her into the forest.

They emerged from the encampment into open ground. Where were they taking her? Their chief, the fat woman Greffa, had ordered that she be taken to a high place. What did she mean by a high place? A mountain? A cliff? How far was the high place? Was there any possibility she might escape before they reached it?

I will show no weakness!

They were heading for a hill. The high place ordered by Greffa was a hill, not particularly high and sufficiently close to the dark forest for her desperate plan to work. If she could somehow break loose, even for a moment, she could run for the dark forest like a gazelle. They would chase after her, of course, but the distance was so short, she was certain she could outrun them. She would have to outrun them—her life depended on it.

And they would not follow her into the forest. Of that she was certain. There were dangers in the forest, as there were dangers everywhere, but there were also monsters in the forest. Not even the arrogant Barradik would dare to face the monsters.

And if they did, a small voice whispered, what of that? There were a thousand places for her to hide in the forest if they dared to venture after her. And if they dared to venture after her, perhaps the monsters would get them. She came close to smiling at the thought.

"This way, girl!" screamed one of the guards, dragging her around.

It was the hill. It had to be the hill. It was the only high place close by, and surely they would wish to kill her close by. She noticed some of the crowd were running ahead in their excitement to see her die.

To her surprise, her guards jerked her to a halt just short of the lower slope. The crowd stopped as well, even those who had run ahead. Shiva waited, wondering what would happen next. A horrid thought occurred to her: What if they bound her before the stoning? If they bound her, she would have no opportunity to attempt escape.

Her whole body ached from the beatings, and the wound on her knee still oozed blood. But she showed nothing of her concern and waited, stoic as a beast. After a moment she saw the reason for the halt. The elders were coming, their purple faces solemn, headed by the chieftain Greffa, who had condemned her. To Shiva's surprise, she noted far more purple faces than had sat in judgment. But however many elders there were made no difference now. The halt had been called to allow them to be first to climb the hill.

They climbed the hill in a spiral path, in single file, watched by the spreading remainder of their tribe. The hill was flat topped, its summit a broad, uneven plateau, barren save for a few stunted shrubs. When the elders reached it, they formed a wide circle. Shiva knew at once who would be at the center of that circle. Her death was to be transformed into a show, and Greffa and her cronies wanted to see it all.

With the elders in position, the remainder of the tribe surged forward, carrying Shiva and her guards along with them. The excitement was explosive now. The crowd had become an animal with a thousand mouths but just one throat and just one appetite. It hummed and buzzed and howled like a single entity. She glanced from face to face and saw the same glittering eyes, the same flaring nostrils, the same mindless intensity. There was lust in the air, and the lust was for her blood.

The two burly guards struck out viciously to clear

a space, obviously uncaring whom they hurt or how much. But those pressing close leaped out of the way with a nimble surefootedness that showed experience of similar situations before. As the passageway was cleared, Shiva was dragged forward, up the hill.

Eventually she reached the top and was pushed violently between two elders so that she staggered into the middle of the circle.

She spun around like a trapped animal. The guards had not even entered the circle. No one held her. But the elder women stood shoulder to shoulder, watching her with frozen faces. And behind them, densely packed, were warriors and women of the tribe, jostling, pushing, standing on tiptoe to get a better view. They spilled down the hill, covering it as densely as a swarm of bees will sometimes cover the branch of a tree before they find themselves a new home. And not just the hill: The Barradik spread out across the surrounding plain, hundreds upon hundreds of them, waiting breathlessly to watch her death. So this was the reason the execution had been ordered on a high place—it meant that everyone could see.

It meant too that there was no escape. Should she run now, she might get past the elders, for

157

many, like their chieftain, were flabby and looked as though they might not move too fast. But getting past the elders was not enough. Getting past the elders would leave her in the middle of the crowd; and judging by the expressions on those hate-filled faces, they would take pleasure in tearing her apart like wolves.

What to do? Since she was dead in any case, Shiva dashed forward anyway, heading directly for the fat chieftain Greffa. But Greffa moved more quickly than Shiva would have believed possible, caught her up and flung her back into the middle of the circle. There was a ragged burst of cheering and much laughter, but no face showed surprise. Obviously she was not the first prisoner to attempt to break free. And such attempts, it seemed, were all part of the entertainment.

Shiva froze into immobility. She would give them no more sport. *She would show no weakness!*

For a moment the elders waited, possibly hoping she would make another run. Shiva stared at them blankly. Her arms hung by her sides. She breathed deeply, withdrawing her mind from the pain so that her legs would not tremble and they not think her afraid. Nothing. She would show nothing. If there was nothing left for her but death, she could at least deprive them of their entertainment.

No weakness. I will show no weakness!

There was a rumble of distant thunder, heralding a storm. Greffa bent down and picked up a stone.

17

Flight of the Crone

I am growing old, the Crone thought. She was laying down a fourth fur, creating a soft pallet on the dry floor of the cave.

The cave was full of magic: goat horns, ram horns, elk skulls, leopard hides, mammoth tusks, claws strung on gut, reindeer antlers, rhino horn, bat wings, crocodile teeth, polished stones, lion fangs—all scattered without order as if blown by a great wind, or dropped like the boulders left by Mamar when his ice sheets retreated northward in the summer.

Behind these tools of a mystic trade were plants, some in wrappings, some in piles, some in bunches, all carefully dried. There seemed as little order here as there was among the horns and tusks and bones.

There was a fire in the cave, lighted in a cleft

that formed a natural chimney at the back. It had burned low, without flames, but an updraft kept the embers glowing dully. As the Crone moved, she cast a monstrous shadow on the cavern walls, like some sinister, gigantic bird.

She reached down to test the softness of the furs. *I am growing old*, she thought again. Once she would have danced to call her spirit guide, danced tirelessly, hour on hour, head bobbing, arms flapping in imitation of its movements. Now arthritis often pained her back and hip and the spirit dance was quite beyond her. No matter. So long as she had enough furs and her magic plants, she still could fly.

With her bed prepared, she slipped a doeskin pouch from her clothing and moved to the scattered store of herbs. Dried plants, shredded leaves, aromatic shavings, petals all went into the pouch, stirred and mixed relentlessly by the Crone's slim fingers. She scarcely looked toward the plants she took, although many—perhaps even most—were poisonous if eaten.

Finally she had enough. The pouch bulged like a well-fed snake. She tied the neck and rolled it vigorously between her hands so that the contents crumbled finely. Then she walked to the cleft, re-opened the pouch, and sprinkled a handful of the roughly powdered herbs onto the fire. A thick plume of greenish smoke curled upward, filling the whole cave with a heavy, narcotic scent.

She leaned forward and inhaled once, deeply, then returned to her bed of furs, picking up a small bone on the way. The smoke billowed after her, so that the interior of the cave became a haze. She knelt carefully—mindful of her hip, although she had been fortunate in that it had not troubled her in days—then lay down on her back on the furs. No chill reached her from the stone beneath.

For a moment she stared up at the roof, then closed her eyes. The taste of the smoke was still strong in her mouth, reinforced by the scent that pervaded the cave. She began to breathe deeply, in through her nose, out through her mouth, counting to her own heartbeat. Her hand, moving almost of its own accord, tapped the bone against the cavern floor, producing a clear, sharp click.

Old, she thought, *but not too old*.

Click, the bone went. *Click . . . click-click . . . click . . . click-click . . . click.*

When the rhythm was established, she began to hum as softly as a single bee in summer, picking up the clicking beat. The sound relaxed her so that her pains and aches began to slide away and her whole body seemed to be growing heavy, aided by

162

the narcotic smoke. The heaviness was pleasant, comfortable and warm.

Her body grew more heavy still. She could feel it sinking sensually into the pile of furs. Then the warmth and relaxation flowed from her shoulders down her arms so that she could no longer lift them.

Her head grew heavy as her neck relaxed. Her mouth dropped open, like that of one in a deep sleep. But she was not asleep.

Click . . . click-click . . . click . . . click-click . . . click.

The rhythm of the clicking swelled to fill her until it seemed there was nothing but the sharp, staccato sound reaching to the farthest corners of the world. Behind her closed eyelids, the Crone watched. She could see the hard, chill, stony land beyond her cave, see the camp of her people and the people within. For a moment she watched the movements of the tribe, the daily routine of fire making, food gathering, meat cutting, shelter building. Then she cast her attention upward.

Click . . . click-click . . . click . . . click-click . . . click.

For a moment the gray sky was empty. Then, with her inner sight, she saw the bird, a large black crow that circled the encampment beneath in search of carrion or any other scraps the tribe might drop.

Click . . . click-click . . . click . . . click-click . . . click.

Eyes still closed, the Crone smiled slightly. Most women in the tribe imagined her totem was the great black bear so beloved of all the magic-making Crones, but while Bear often came to her in dreams and spoke to her and helped her in her work, her spirit guardian had always been a creature of a different type, more subtle and in certain ways more sinister. On the day of her initiation, when she had made the journey into the lower world, it was Crow who greeted her.

Now the clicking called on Crow again; and Crow replied, as Crow always replied, signaling her presence by the appearance of a natural crow.

For a moment the Crone watched the soaring swooping of the bird with her inner eye, then drew deep within herself in preparation. The sensation was as frightening as always, but she ignored the fear. She gathered her consciousness into a tight ball behind her eyes and held it there, summoning her will and strength. Then, with a massive effort, she hurled it upward.

She felt a rush of movement, then the familiar blinding wrench as she hurtled from her body. This was the worst part, a naked vulnerability that created its own terror and convinced her, each time, that she was close to death. Her mind writhed and spun, and tried to fly for shelter. For an instant all was panic, but she fought her fear with all the skill produced by years of practice, fought, and conquered it. She rode the rhythm of the clicking: *Click . . . click-click . . . click . . . click-click . . . click.*

The soaring crow cried once more in sudden alarm.

The Crone opened her eyes.

She was inside the crow.

She could see the camp below her, the women of the tribe scuttling back and forth like ants. She could see the cliff face where her woman's body lay on its bed of furs within the cave. She could see so much with the crow's eyes, so much sharp detail lost to human sight, especially old and failing human sight.

But that was not the best of it. The best of it was the sudden freedom from pain, the sensation of speed and power, above all the ability to fly! This was the greatest freedom of them all. However often experienced, it never ceased to thrill her. She soared and dived, tumbled, swerved and soared again. A raucous cry tore from her unfamiliar tongue, announcing pure joy to the land and sky.

Eventually she slowed in her gyrations, listening to a call of duty too strong to be ignored. With strong, steady beats of her powerful wings, she climbed up, higher and higher, but purposefully now. Below she could see the sweep of the countryside, made unfamiliar by perspective. There was the cliff face, marching northward. There was the village camp sprawled below her, so insignificantly tiny now that she could no longer make out individual members of the tribe. There was the river, a silver serpent winding its coils around rocks and hills and clumps of trees. There, distant, was the water hole where Shiva sometimes went to wash.

The Crone turned her head to stare with one black and glittering eye toward the water hole. Each time she left her ancient body to take the body of a crow, her senses sharpened so acutely, it seemed she could see faint intimations of the past or future. And there was something at the water hole, a group of tantalizing shapes, writhing, fading and re-forming at the edge of consciousness. They had no solidity, no reality; and yet they had the smell of Barradik. Somehow she knew that what had happened at the water hole impinged on her concerns. Shiva had been there. Now Shiva was gone, taken by the Barradik. In her bird body, the

Crone turned in the direction of the distant Bar-radik encampment.

The air was chill, as the air was always chill, yet she felt no real cold. Bird feathers were an excellent insulation, even in the worst of weather, and the effort of flight warmed her. Looking down, she saw the rocky terrain passing beneath her, unfamiliar until her mind recognized the new perspective. She saw the smooth movement of an auroch herd, the animals far less ungainly from above than they were when seen on the ground. She saw the sweep of the plain and, distantly, the looming darkness of the great forest, hiding its strange masters.

She flew with joy, remembering her mission, yet light and pain-free in the body of her totem bird. The world below her was a wonder now, bright and fresh as morning dew, as if seen for the first time. She flew swiftly, far faster than a hunter trots, perhaps faster even than the steed she had given to Renka. She flew straight, uncaring of the obstacles below. She felt free.

Sounds reached her: the lowing bellow of cattle, the *click-click* of a goat's hooves on rock, the roar of distant water as it poured into a pool. She swooped low over the graceful form of a large black hunting cat. The animal heard the powerful beating of her wings and looked up in alarm.

A herd of mammoth stretched beneath her, the largest she had ever seen. The great beasts were so numerous, they created a woolly carpet that undulated strangely on the plain beneath. She wondered briefly why so many had gathered at one time. Perhaps these creatures held their own Star Jamboree in honor of the Mother.

Flying with untiring ease, the Crone climbed higher and increased her speed until, quite quickly now, her destination was in sight. Close by the dark forest, like a spreading bloodstain on the plain, was the Barradik encampment, row upon row of black and filthy yurts, the deaths of ten thousand animals commemorated in those skin tents. The Crone's eyes narrowed. She had no cause to condemn the Barradik, she of all people who had killed often—aye, and not only animals. Yet the deaths she had caused had all been for a purpose, all served—so she hoped—a greater good. But the Barradik were different. The Barradik were careless of death. They killed with far too little thought, and this was an abomination.

She was still thinking with disgust of the Barradik when she saw Shiva.

The Crone stopped on the instant, hanging motionless in the air above the blood camp, her wings lightly beating to hold her position. Mob sounds

168

welled up from below, and men and women like ants poured from the encampment, streaming toward a nearby hill. They had a small figure at their head, a figure held and dragged like a prisoner or one condemned. Although too far away to see the features, the Crone's newly sharpened senses told her instantly that this was Shiva. The Barradik were taking the girl to the hill.

She watched, coldly calm, with preternatural patience. She knew enough of Barradik custom to suspect what might be happening, but she wanted to be sure. She felt the vile excitement of the crowd, welling up like a noxious fog to insult the Mother in the dreamtime. Shiva was limping slightly, although she hid it well.

The guards jerked her to a halt at the base of the hill, so violently that she almost stumbled. The Crone flew closer, dropping down until she hovered above the heads of the mob. Shiva was bruised and cut, as if from a bad beating. Blood oozed from one leg, and though she stood straight and tall, still there was a trembling of the muscles that spoke of near exhaustion. A chilling knot of hatred grew within the Crone's heart. The Barradik would pay, she thought. Whatever their motives for this atrocity, the Barradik would pay!

A movement caught her eye, and she saw the

processional approach of the Barradik elders, their purple faces solemn. It told her what she wished to know. This was, without a doubt, an execution, a stoning on the high ground, in accordance with Barradik custom. The elder women would surround their victim and the chieftain, Greffa, would have the privilege of throwing the first stone.

It required little wisdom to guess who the victim would be.

Moving with stately deliberation, the procession of elders started up the hill. The Crone watched them for a moment more, black eyes glittering with abhorrence; then she wheeled and flew, faster even than before. She guided her flight with great deliberation. They would pay, those creatures down there by the hill. They had taken the girl Shiva and the girl Shiva belonged to her, the Crone. None knew this yet, not even Shiva, yet it was so. And those who sought to harm this child must answer to the Crone. How they would pay, these Barradik. How they would pay for their abominations!

In no more than moments, the Crone reached the vast herd of grazing mammoth, passed above them to land, light as thistledown, on the plain beyond. With a half-conscious movement, she wrapped her wings around her and strutted toward the nearest bull. The great beast continued to graze, unaware of her presence.

The Crone stopped, so close to the creature that three short hops would have left her perching on the curving tusks. She watched it for a moment, bobbing her head to take in the immensity of the beast. Then she began to withdraw deep into the body of the bird. Sensing a lessening of her control, the crow tried to fly away, but found it could not and groomed the pinions of its wings instead.

With her consciousness enfolded layer upon layer like some glittering ball, the Crone commenced to croon softly within her mind, a discordant song full of uneasy rhythms. After a moment, the mammoth bull looked about it nervously.

The song of the Crone continued, a silent thing that somehow crawled upon the air and wormed its way into the mind of every creature listening. It carried feathers of fear, tendrils of pure panic, images of snakes and mice.

The mammoth trumpeted a sudden warning.

The Crone sang, triumphantly.

There were answering trumpets as the alarm was taken up by other bulls throughout the herd. All the beasts, as far as she could see, had ceased their grazing now and were standing, heads raised, turning back and forth as they sought to discover the nature of the danger.

The Crone's song climbed in pitch, increased in its discordancy. It held the scream of a rabbit caught in an eagle's claws, the howl of a wolf, the screech of tortured spirits. It held death and terror. She took off and flew, releasing the full horror of her song.

Below, the mammoth milled in panic, churning the ground with their great feet. Then, with a rumble like thunder, the herd began to move.

18

Disaster at the Camp

It was Renka! There was no mistaking the boar skin, the sturdy, square-set body, although her face was so puffed and pale and streaked with blood as to be virtually unrecognizable. But it was Renka astride a horse—a nightmare impossibility. At least it had been Renka astride a horse. She had decently fallen off now, and was lying on the ground staring up at him with dull, unseeing eyes.

Hiram watched her, half crouched, as he sometimes watched particularly dangerous prey. She had definitely been seated on the horse, seated upright, legs clasping its sides, hands holding its mane. And the horse had not thrown her. She had slid from its back like one far gone in illness or exhaustion, but the horse had not minded her at all—still did not mind her now, but stood close by her, eying Hiram warily.

This had the smell of sorcery, of Cronecraft. Hiram shivered. It was unnatural that a human being should sit astride a horse, unnatural that the creature should carry her. Cronecraft for sure. The Crone would dare the anger of the Mother Goddess herself as she pursued her dark magic.

Renka groaned.

Hiram took a step toward her, then hesitated. The horse worried him. It was a small-enough creature, a pony really, and a mare rather than a stallion, but it was a wild animal all the same. The Crone's witchcraft might protect the chieftain while she was seated on its back, but Hiram was far from certain the magic would extend to him if he approached too near. Horses were dangerous beasts, more dangerous in some respects than hunting cats, which generally avoided humankind. Horses were prey, hence nervous, prone to lashing out with fore and hind feet at the mildest provocation. Only two summers before, one of the hunt had been kicked to death by a pony just a little larger than this one. It had caught him on the side of the head and crushed his skull.

All the same, this mare seemed unusually placid. While she had watched him earlier, she seemed to have decided he was harmless now and turned away, snuffling on the rocky ground for a tuft of grass. Perhaps he might approach safely, after all.

Renka groaned again and the sound turned to a terrifying rattle in her throat. Hiram moved to her at once and the pony only danced away a few short steps, making no attempt at all to lash out. He ignored it and reached for Renka, that rattle still echoing in his mind. As a hunter, he had seen enough accidents to know she was close to death. But how?

Her eyes rolled upward, showing only the whites, turning her face into a hideous mask.

"Forgive me, Lady," Hiram muttered and pushed his hand inside her furs onto her breast. For a moment he thought she must be dead, then faintly, beneath his palm, he felt the fluttering of her heart, like a wounded bird.

She smelled of blood. Something made him pull back the skins that covered her thighs and there he saw the wounds. She had been raked by one of the great cats, and raked cruelly. He stared at the wounds in bewilderment. The cats so seldom attacked people that he scarcely knew what to do. Much of the blood had dried now, but one of the wounds spurted feebly in a horrid rhythm. The sight chilled him. He had seen such wounds before.

If the blood flow was not stopped it led to death.

Unwilling to tear his leader's clothing, Hiram ripped a strip from one of his own furs and wrapped it quickly round her leg, high up on the thigh. He knotted it clumsily, then looked around until he found a short length of stick, which he pushed through the loop and twisted savagely. The bleeding stopped. He stared at the wound dully. Stopped now, but was his action too late? Renka was no longer conscious, her breathing ragged. She needed far more expert ministrations than he could give her. She needed the Crone. But the Crone was far away, many hours' march, in the encampment. Renka could no longer stand upright, let alone walk such a distance.

He glanced at the shaggy pony, but dismissed the half-formed thought. Even if the beast would carry her, it would certainly not carry him, so who was there to guide it where it had to go? No, Chief Renka would have to recover here. He bent and picked her up bodily, at once wondering at how light she was, much lighter than he had expected. He carried her across to the shelter of a rock crevice and made her as comfortable as he was able. She looked deathly pale, waxy cold and corpselike already, but there was nothing more he could do for her. Chief Renka would recover here, or die. There was nothing more he could do.

And, his mind reminded him, no time to do it in even if there were. He had to rescue Shiva.

Hiram trotted from the shelter of the rocks, moving forward even as an empty sickness descended like a winter pall upon his soul. What could he do? He was one and one alone against the entire Barradik nation. Shiva was captured, beaten, guarded, surrounded. What could one man do? Shiva was taken . . .

In his heart, Hiram knew Shiva was taken to her execution.

All the same, there had to be something he could do, and his hunter's lore convinced him there was always hope, however slim. In his yellow-faced and feather-haired disguise, he slipped unobtrusively into the tail of the mob procession moving toward the hill. As the smell of the Barradik surrounded him, he wondered at his own courage, for he knew what would happen were he to be discovered. Except that it was not courage at all, but desperation. He could not imagine an existence with Shiva dead.

Besides, there was little real danger. If he stayed silent and drew no attention to himself, his presence in the crowd would never be noticed. Really, he was as safe here as he would have been in his home encampment with the ringfires lit.

Except, a small voice reminded him reasonably, if he stayed quiet and drew no attention to himself, he could hardly hope to rescue Shiva.

The mob was milling around the foot of a small hill, jostling and laughing in an air of expectation that reminded Hiram of the tension before a thunderstorm. One thickset warrior bumped into him and snarled an angry curse. Hiram bit back his instinctive reaction, averted his eyes and remained silent, heart pounding. The man, fortunately, decided to make nothing more of it and pushed away into the crowd. Hiram stood tall and looked for Shiva.

She was held by two thin guards, surrounded by several more. Her features were expressionless; she stood straight and paid attention neither to her guards nor to the crowd around her. Those closest were jeering her as a Shingu whelp, and one woman actually spat at her but missed, catching a guard on the arm.

Carefully, so as not to anger anyone and thus draw attention to himself, Hiram began to edge his way through the crowd. He still had no plan, but he knew he must be close to Shiva if he was to aid her to escape. Except, that reasonable voice in his mind insisted, there could be no possible escape from this situation. She was guarded.

The mob fell suddenly silent. Heads turned, and as Hiram followed the communal gaze, he saw the slow, measured approach of a serpentine procession: women with purple faces, features grim but eyes alight with anticipation, the tribal elders of the Barradik. The crowd parted to let them pass and they walked, eyes firmly fixed ahead, only a few paces from where Hiram was standing. He recognized the portly figure of Greffa, the Barradik chieftain, at the head; and close to her two others he remembered from their visit to Renka, although he could not recall their names.

The elder procession circled the hill, then climbed it in a spiral path. The crowd fell in behind the last of the purple-painted women, Hiram with them. By chance his position was perfect, so that by the time they reached the flat top of the hill, he was no more than an arm's reach from the circle formed by the elders, so close to Shiva now that he could have called out words of encouragement and she would certainly have heard him. But he remained silent and only stared, his mind a brutal turmoil. They planned to stone her—that much was clear. And if he did not do something soon, it would be too late. But what to do? *What to do?*

The mob fell silent, so that distantly he heard the sound of rolling thunder, like the approach of an ominous storm. The guards drew back from Shiva so that she stood, a solitary figure, in the center of the elder circle. Mindlessly, Hiram moved forward until he was pressed against the back of an elder woman. He must act now. *Now!*

Chieftain Greffa bent suddenly and picked up a stone about the size of an eagle's egg. She weighed it in her hand, smiling a little. She looked toward Shiva.

Now! Hiram pushed hard against the elder in front of him. She turned angrily and snapped a brittle command for him to step back. A red haze was forming on the edges of Hiram's vision and he groped for his club. The storm seemed to be getting nearer, for the thunder was louder now, unless it was blood pounding in his ears.

Shiva turned slightly to stare into the eyes of Greffa. She held her head proudly and there was no fear in her face. Greffa's smile widened and she drew back her arm.

Hiram struck the elder in front of him viciously, driving the head of his club into the pit of her stomach. The breath exploded violently from her lungs and a look of pained surprise passed across her features. Then she doubled forward. Hiram, half mad with panic now, struck her again on the back of the head so that she pitched forward, unconscious. Expecting to be seized at any moment, he leaped across the prostrate body.

Greffa hurled the stone.

Hiram had broken through the circle. The elder he had hit lay facedown, blood oozing from the fresh head wound. Those on either side were staring down at her in astonishment. There was a great noise of thunder now, and he thought he felt a trembling in the ground beneath his feet. Somewhere on the distant outskirts of the mob, men began to scream and shout.

Shiva remained impassive, immobile. The stone thrown by Greffa passed by her right cheek, lightly brushing her hair.

Momentum carried Hiram forward, but he stumbled, fought to regain his balance. The thunder was loud in his ears and the ground was definitely trembling now. He caught himself and dropped into a fighting crouch. If Shiva was to die, he would die with her!

He found himself looking at Greffa, but Greffa was not looking at him. She had turned to stare behind her into the crowd. Something was wrong, badly wrong.

The circle of elders broke abruptly, but the mob, instead of pushing inward, seemed to flow away, down the hill. The screams and shouts were louder now and there was a distinct scent of fear in the air. One of the elders, the hideous woman with the scars on her cheeks, shouted loudly, "What is it? What's the matter?"

It was not thunder. It was never thunder! In his entire life, Hiram had never heard a sound like this. It rolled like thunder, but it never ceased, merely grew louder and louder as the crowd disintegrated into panic. He felt a chill hand close upon his heart. Was he listening to the wrath of the Mother? Did she seek to punish the Barradik for what they tried to do to Shiva, who had found the Saber skull? If so, he hoped she would recognize him as Shingu and Shiva's friend beneath his disguise. It would be unendurable if the Mother Goddess killed him thinking he was Barradik.

The crowd was breaking up, milling, screaming, clumps of people breaking away to run down the hill. And suddenly he saw it.

Below, across the plain, the massive herd of mammoth was in full stampede, bearing down on the Barradik encampment like a herald of doom. Trunks raised and trumpeting in fright, the beasts thundered on, a raging torrent of destruction that swept aside bushes, trees, anything in their path. Stunned, Hiram watched. He had never seen such a sight as this. The beasts were a hurtling madness, a thunder roll of terror, trampling, crushing, racing onward.

The herd, he saw at once, was going to miss the hill, if only barely. Those who remained on the high ground would be safe. But the crowd, with all the stupidity of crowds, did not remain on the hill, but poured downward to the low ground and there split, some running away, some, in their insanity, running toward the approaching beasts.

As he watched, the first few Barradik were trampled underfoot. Then an entire clump went down, screaming, a purple-faced elder among them. The mammoth herd rolled on relentlessly, scarcely noticing the tiny human creatures underneath their feet. Nothing slowed it, nothing diverted it. Where a rock rose too high to run across, the herd simply split, flowed round it, then rejoined again to thunder on.

Dozens, scores of Barradik were already dead, more dying all the time. Then the stampede struck the yurt encampment like a tidal wave.

Hiram had thought the entire Barradik nation was on or near the hill to watch the death of Shiva. Now he realized he could scarcely have been more wrong. Many had poured out to watch the execution, yet many, many more remained. He saw them now, fleeing screaming in panic before the mammoth, which smashed yurts as if they were no more than brittle tinder.

The fires started as he watched, flowering in one collapsed yurt, then another. The sight of flames increased the panic in the camp: Those few women who tried to organize water found their shouted orders ignored. Hiram found himself wondering if the fires would turn the mammoths, for all creatures save humankind and ogres feared fire. But the great beasts were beyond turning. They raced trumpeting through the entire encampment, breaking down everything in their path. And the fire crawled through the debris, now strong enough to leap the gaps, beginning to crackle and roar, bringing pain and death to those it ringed and trapped.

Hiram watched with horrid fascination, unable to tear his eyes away from the disaster. The screams and cries of the Barradik blended until they seemed like the death calls of some vast, multiheaded creature of the dreamtime. And still the slaughter continued: men, women, children trampled underfoot or caught in the spreading flames.

He saw the edges of the mammoth herd pour

through the rocky stretch of ground where he had left Chief Renka and chilled at the thought of his leader trampled. But there was nothing he could do now, nothing anyone could do to stop the herd. The mammoth were like a blizzard or a flood, an earthquake or an avalanche, an act of nature that had to be avoided or endured, but could not be changed in any way. Was Renka dead? He could not see her from the hill and he had left her sheltered. Could it be that she survived?

The crowd was draining away, running, screaming, howling its fear in a voice that actually climbed above the noise of the stampede and the increasing roar of the flames that now threatened to engulf the entire camp. It was a disaster such as no human tribe had faced before, death and destruction of almost unimaginable magnitude. Yet he could not find it in his heart to pity the Barradik, who had treated the Shingu with such arrogance, who had taken Shiva to kill her.

Shiva! Now, while disaster struck, he had at last the opportunity to rescue Shiva! He spun around, searching for her, calling for her. There was no reply, no sign. He was alone on the hill.

19
Death of Shiva

Renka opened her eyes. She was aware of her body, but only dimly, for her mind floated like a leaf on a stream. Somewhere, distantly, there was stiffness and pain, but it had little to do with her. She felt weak and warm and happy.

She was not quite certain where she was, although she seemed to be inside a cave. Lights danced and flickered, casting shadows on the walls, and when, slowly, she turned her head, she saw the glow of a fire, cunningly built into a rock cleft so that the smoke was carried upward.

There was much else in the cave. Her eyes moved with slow curiosity across an array of skulls and bones and heaps of dried and wizened plants. From the plants came the smell, an aroma of herbs that pervaded the air and helped her float. She smiled a little at the thought that she was floating.

She wondered where she was, but without urgency. She was warm and free—or almost free—from pain. She closed her eyes again and tried to move to make herself more comfortable. Momentarily, the pain drew closer, concentrating in her leg and thigh. It flared for an instant, sharp and bright, then died away again to a dull, pulsating ache.

Brief though it had been, the flare brought memories. Strange memories. It seemed she had ridden on a horse. It was ridiculous, of course, yet she seemed clearly to remember she had ridden on a horse and the horse had carried her like the wind. Perhaps the memory was a dream. But if she had dreamed the horse, then she must have dreamed the other thing as well, the attack by the lioness who raked her leg. And if she had only dreamed the lioness, then why was she in pain? She opened her eyes again, thinking to inspect her thigh.

She was looking into the black, glittering eyes of the Crone.

"Do you see me, Renka?" asked the Crone.

"I see you, Sister," Renka said. "Where am I?"

"In my cave," the Crone said quietly.

Another memory arose, floating unbidden from the depths of her mind. "I was attacked by a Bar-

187

radik," Renka said. She could see him still, yellow-faced and evil, standing over her with a club.

"You are safe now," the Crone assured her.

"I was attacked by a lioness as well," Renka said.

The Crone nodded. "I know."

Renka closed her eyes and smiled. "The magic pony carried me away from the cat," she said. She wanted to ask about the magic pony, but her lips and tongue would no longer function and her mind grew confused and dim and she sank, without effort, into darkness.

When she awoke again, the pain was sharper, more pronounced, but at least her head was clear. She was still in the cave, the Crone's cave—the Crone's magic cave, where none might enter. She saw the bones and skulls and herbs and other artifacts of Cronecraft and wondered that she was permitted to see such things. The fire in the chimney cleft had burned low, was now little more than a pile of glowing embers, but gray daylight was filtering from somewhere so that she could see quite well.

She turned her head and found to her astonishment that the young man Hiram was squatting by the entrance watching her with a hunter's patience. At her movement he rose at once and ran from the cave.

She was lying, she discovered, on a bed of furs, covered with more furs, heavy and malodorous, but warm. There was an ache in her back, her shoulders and her arms. Her leg felt as if it had taken fire.

Renka pushed herself into a sitting position. At once the pain burst upon her with such violence that the entire cavern reeled and spun. She clamped her teeth and concentrated her strength and waited. Eventually, slowly, the pain receded, leaving her shaking, sweating, but once more in control. She sat upright, breathing deeply, waiting for strength, considering her next move.

The Crone slid silently through the crevice entrance. "Lie down, Renka!" she said sharply. "You are not well enough to move."

Renka lay, moving cautiously so that she should not again provoke the intensity of pain, but turned on her elbow so that she could still see the Crone. "I have been ill, Lady Witch?" she asked formally.

"You have been close to death," the Crone said bluntly. She approached the pallet and squatted, staring at Renka with the eyes of a spider watching her prey. "Too close for the good of our nation," she added sourly, as if the matter were no one's fault but Renka's own.

"I am growing stronger now," Renka said. It was

true: She did feel stronger. Not yet strong, but stronger. Something of her old power came back, and she said firmly, "You had better tell me what happened."

"What happened?" the Crone echoed grimly. "Much has happened—much. Shall I tell you how a thousand Barradik were killed? Or how their entire encampment was destroyed? Shall I tell you of the stampede of beasts, or the lioness who savaged you?"

"Where is the pony?" Renka asked. The mare had carried her far from home, and in her weakness she had fallen from its back. Something rose up from her breast to clutch tightly at her throat: There was a special horror in the thought that she might have lost the magic pony now.

But the Crone's expression softened. "She returned."

"Who rode her?"

"No one rode her—she returned on her own."

Renka blinked. "How did she find her way back?"

"As any creature finds its way," the Crone said inscrutably.

"Is she—" Renka hesitated, then plunged on. "Is she hurt?"

"A lot less than you are," the Crone said dryly.

Then she gave the smallest of smiles. "She is well and uninjured. Even now she grazes in the grove."

Renka lay back, astonished how relieved she felt. So much she needed to know. How long had she lain ill? Was Shiva safe? What had happened? Yet with all the questions that tumbled through her mind, the one she had asked first, the one that gave her such relief, had concerned an animal she scarcely knew. Perhaps, she thought, she scarcely knew herself as well.

She opened her mouth to ask about Shiva, but the Crone had begun to speak. "There is much you truly need to know," she said. "I talk to you as chieftain now. Is your mind cleared?"

Renka nodded. "Yes." It was true. Her body still felt weak, but she was in control of herself again. In a way she was almost sorry. The floating sensation had been very pleasant.

"It seems," the Crone said, "you were attacked by a lion."

Renka nodded. "There were two. I think they were after the mare." A thought struck her. "They did not injure her?"

The Crone shook her head impatiently. "She had no wounds, not even old wounds. The cat clawed you, not the mare."

"I remember. But the mare ran fast and carried me away."

"Doubtless," the Crone said dryly. "But you lost much blood—that much was obvious when I saw you. You talked a great deal while you were healing. Not much of it made sense, but from what you said and what I learned, you reached the Barradik encampment—or close to it. By the time you did so, you were close to death. You fell from the horse. You might have died on the ground."

"I saw a Barradik warrior," Renka put in, frowning.

"You saw the hunter Hiram with yellow paint on his face and black feathers in his hair," the Crone said shortly.

Renka looked at her. "Painted like a Barradik? But why?"

The Crone shrugged. "Who knows what goes on in the minds of young men?" She sniffed. "Especially such a one as that. He visits a marula grove, he sees ogres, he paints his face yellow." She shrugged again. "Be happy, Renka. He saved your life."

"It was so?"

"It was so. He stopped the flow of blood. His work was crude. He would never make a healer. But at least he stopped the flow. Then he placed you in shelter between rocks. Thus you did not die. Later, following the destruction, he came for you and found you and brought you back to me."

"I lay in darkness, close to death," Renka said. "How did he bring me back to you?"

With no change of expression, the Crone said, "He carried you."

"Carried—?" Renka stared in astonishment. The distance was enormous, much of it over rough ground.

The Crone nodded again. "He is a young fool, but in some ways he is a remarkable young fool."

"I thought I saw him here earlier, just after I awoke," Renka said.

"He was here. I set him to watch over you, charged him to alert me at once should you waken."

After a moment, Renka said, "No man may enter the cave of a Crone."

The Crone sniffed. "I made that rule, thus I may break it. This is not important, Chief Renka. What is important is what has happened and what will happen. What has happened is that the Barradik encampment has been utterly destroyed. Many, many Barradik have been killed. Women, men, children. Hundreds, perhaps thousands."

Thunderstruck, Renka struggled to a sitting position, ignoring the sudden violent jabs of pain. "How?"

"An act of the Mother Goddess," the Crone told her blandly. "Their camp was trampled by a stampede of mammoth." She reached out and placed a firm hand on Renka's chest to encourage her to lie down again.

Renka subsided, her heart pounding. "They were evil, the Barradik. It was a judgment. Now our totem will be chosen."

"A judgment? Perhaps. Perhaps not. But whatever it was, the Barradik remain the threat they have always been. However many were killed, they are still as numerous as the sands of the shore, still as powerful. Their leader survived and all her inner council, all but one of the extended council."

"Was the Giant's Thighbone destroyed?"

"They say not," the Crone said.

"So the Hag still must choose at the Star Jamboree?"

"The Hag is dead," the Crone said flatly.

This time Renka sat up fluidly, her pain suppressed by shock. She actually waved away the Crone's restraining hand. "Dead?" she echoed. "The Hag is *dead*?"

"Before a new totem is chosen, a new Hag must be chosen."

194

Suddenly very much afraid, but not knowing why, Renka whispered, "You, Sister? You shall be Hag?"

The Crone nodded.

Thinking always of the tribe, Renka said, "But who shall be our Crone?"

"There are matters more urgent, Chief Renka. I have told you the Hag is dead. I did not tell you how she died, nor did you ask."

Renka frowned. "She was old, the oldest woman I have ever seen."

"Yet old age did not claim her. She was murdered."

There was a long moment's silence in the cave. Eventually Renka breathed. "Who did this thing?"

"They will say I did," the Crone said calmly. "Or some other Shingu. They will say it was done in order that the Skull of Saber become the next Star Totem."

"They would not dare!"

"It is already being said. This is the reason why the Barradik took Shiva."

Renka stared at her. "I do not understand you, Sister."

The Crone leaned forward. "Understand this," she said impatiently. "The Barradik took Shiva because they say she murdered the Hag."

"Shiva murdered the Hag? Is this what they claim?"

"This is what they claim. This is why they took her. Tomorrow when the nations gather for the great Star Jamboree—"

"Tomorrow?" screamed Renka. "How long have I lain ill?"

"Many days and many nights."

"The Star Jamboree is *tomorrow*?"

"Tomorrow," the Crone repeated. "And tomorrow Greffa will tell the nations that the Hag was murdered by a Shingu and the Shingu tribe will be an abomination in the eyes of the nations."

"They will not believe her!"

"They will believe," said the Crone grimly. "For will not I—a Shingu—be chosen as the new Hag? And will not I, as Hag, select the Shingu Skull of Saber for Star Totem? And will Greffa not accuse Shiva, a Shingu, who found the Skull of Saber, of the old Hag's murder? They will hear these things and they will believe. Surely they will believe. You see why I speak to you as leader, Renka—tomorrow will bring the greatest threat our tribe has ever faced."

"But Shiva could not have killed the Hag. She is a girl, little more than a child!" She trailed off, her eyes fixed on the Crone's stony face. "Where is Shiva, Sister?"

The Crone said, "She is dead. Hiram carried back the news. She was trampled by the mammoth herd while fleeing from the Barradik."

20
Hiram Mourns

The village was in turmoil. With bustle, fuss and noise, the Shingu tribe made departure preparations for the Star Jamboree. Women shouted orders. Men, women, children all scurried here and there intent on different tasks. They were a nomad people, well accustomed to breaking camp and moving to follow the migrating game, but this time it was different. This time it was a move so complex and demanding that it required every ounce of effort and organization the tribe possessed.

At other times the tribe traveled light, taking no more than their clothing, their weapons, a handful of important artifacts and themselves. Many minor totems, building materials and tools were left stored in deep caves or buried near the traditional campsites, ready for use when the tribe returned.

Even the food supplies they carried were small, unless the weather was particularly bad—for the Shingu hunt was skilled and ensured the tribe could live well off the land.

But the Jamboree was different, for the Jamboree was not held on a Shingu campsite or the campsite of any tribe. Thus the Shingu must carry everything they needed to rebuild their temporary village. And since the Jamboree would last for several days, they were required to bring food to feed themselves— and such guests as they might care to entertain— during that time. Every tribe took part in the celebrations and no hunt went out.

All important magical artifacts had to be carried to the Jamboree. Some were entered as candidates for Star Totem. Those not entered were used in the secret meetings of the Crones. Many tools and furs and hides were carried to the Jamboree for barter, as were supplies of red and yellow ocher.

And there was always something new. At the last Star Jamboree, two southern tribes arrived with leather containers full of fermented fruit pulp, made, so it was whispered, by adding marula pulp to beaten fruit. There had been many who feared to taste the mixture, for marula was a gift of the Goddess, not to be mixed with any other fruit. But those who did drink and chewed the mixture reported that while it was sour to the tongue, still it contained the burning magic.

There was great prestige in bringing something new to a Star Jamboree, for if the new thing proved popular, it might be bartered for wealth, sometimes great wealth. To bring a new thing that was popular was almost as good as having a tribal totem chosen as Star Totem.

This year, the Shingu had the Skull of Saber, which (so everyone was certain) must be chosen as Star Totem. But beyond that, they brought a new thing, never seen before by any tribe. The new thing was portable image magic: mystic pictures of game animals painted by the Crone on slate and thus capable of being transported anywhere. The Crone had daubed three images in all—a deer, a boar and an auroch cow—but these had been copied many times by those young women of the tribe who painted the men's faces in time of war. For while only a Crone had the magic to create a new image, the young women had the skill to copy what was already drawn.

There would be great interest in the new, portable image magic, especially since it had been generated by the Shingu Crone, whose dark reputation stood second only to that of the Hag herself. And now, thanks to the young women, there would be many examples of it to barter. But for the moment, the slates were a great trouble since they would break if dropped and so had to be wrapped in skins and carefully carried. One more worry in the heaving mass of problems that accompanied the journey to the Jamboree.

Hiram watched the preparations apathetically. His soul was empty, his heart lay wooden in his chest. Nothing reached him, nothing touched him. His mind hung like a pall of smoke about the death of Shiva.

How could it have happened? He had been so close to her—no more than a few short feet away. Two steps and he might have reached out to hold her in his arms, to safeguard and protect her. Yet when he had turned to her, she was gone.

Hiram had relived the horror of the moment a thousand times since then; and he relived it now. He could hear the thunder of the mammoth stampede, the screams and shouts of the Barradik, the crackle of flames from the Barradik camp. All was noise and nightmare, a jumble of impressions that crowded in on him, swept over him like an avalanche of snow.

So close. He had been so close! Somehow the Mother had favored him so that he had tracked Shiva without difficulty, escaped the mammoth herd, arrived at the Barradik encampment while she remained alive, joined the Barradik mob without detection and finally, incredibly, managed to be there, alert and ready, when the disaster that struck the Barradik permitted him a real chance to rescue her.

So much from the Mother, yet with it all, he had managed to let Shiva die.

In his mind's eye—for he was one of the few Shingu who could do such a thing—he watched himself turn while the mammoth ran and the Barradik screamed. In reality he had turned quickly, but now, in his vision, he turned slowly indeed. In his vision, there seemed to be a whole series of Hirams, one following the other, turning, turning, endlessly turning.

And the hilltop was empty. The Barradik had fled in panic, elders, guards, tribespeople all. Shiva was no longer where she had stood so bravely to face her execution. Hiram was alone.

Alone. The word echoed through his mind like the haunting call of spirits or the reverberating scream of the nightwing. Alone then and alone now. In the midst of his tribe, in the midst of all this bustling activity, he was alone.

Eventually the griefstorm passed. Hiram remembered how he had risen and walked like one possessed, eyes dull, listless and staring, to the rocky place where he had left his leader. He thought Renka too must be dead, for the mammoth had flowed through that area as well, like a torrent of destruction, but some glimmering of his old self, with its fear of women and developed sense of duty, forced him to make sure.

He touched her and knew at once her color was a sign of fever rather than of health. Her whole body burned like the fires of the Barradik camp. Unless he could get help, she was not long for this world.

In the instant, he thought fleetingly of the Barradik. Their Crone would doubtless know the secret of the fever potions and of binding wounds so that they healed clean and sweet. But the Barradik were enemies. The Barradik had tried to kill Shiva—had in fact caused her death as surely as if they had crushed her themselves. However grave her situation, there could be no question of delivering Chief Renka into the hands of the Shingu's enemies. There had to be another way.

The only real help was back at the Shingu camp, but by the time he reached it and guided someone back, Renka would certainly be dead. Had Hiram been a different man—or even the same man at a different time—he might have despaired then. As it was, the small death of his soul had left him near to witless. He reached for Renka, swung her sweating body across his shoulders, and moved off in a stumbling hunter's trot.

He remembered little of the journey, which was, in any case, impossible. Errant images crawled from the dark corners of his mind. He saw himself and his burden fall into a shallow ravine. He waded a stream. He slept fitfully, wrapped around Renka's feverish body for warmth. He limped, one leg dragging. He crawled.

There was one potent image, disconnected with all others: streaks of reddened clouds across a fiery sky, as if the Mother herself had grown angry. And there was snow. Even at this season, there was snow, in light, sharp flurries that left the smallest skim of white on ground and rocks.

He came at last to the camp, mumbling words to no one like an old, old man. His hands were bloody and raw—why or how he could not tell— and his left foot and ankle were swollen nearly twice their normal size. But he still carried his burden, still carried his chief.

Darkness claimed him and he awoke in warmth and darkness in the forbidden cavern of the Crone. So ill was he, it did not even frighten him. And the Crone herself was there, darkly sinister, to feed him a magical, foul-tasting brew and spread a painful poultice of leaves on his foot.

He recovered with amazing speed—the Crone claimed this was because he was young and strong. But the recovery was only in his body. His heart remained empty of all emotions save one.

Hiram angered. Not the hot, healthy, flaring rage of youth that rose up quickly, then was gone, but rather a bitter, cold, gnawing fury that consumed his entire being. It consumed him now, as he watched the preparations, an anger turned toward one person and one only: Greffa, chieftain of the Barradik, the woman who had condemned his beloved Shiva to die.

It was Greffa who led the council that had sentenced Shiva to the hill. It was Greffa who had thrown the first stone. Without Greffa and her filthy tribe, Shiva would have been safe with the Shingu, not lying broken beneath the feet of mammoth.

Streams of porters were already pouring from the camp, carrying ridiculously heavy loads. Although he was fit now and his foot completely healed, Hiram made no move to join in the Jamboree preparations. The tribe, he knew, would march throughout the day to reach their new campsite. And he would march with them. Oh yes, he would certainly march with them. He would help erect the new village. He would play his part in the ceremonies and dances. He would mingle with the people of the other tribes. He would even, though his heart was broken, smile and pretend enjoyment.

And when the opportunity arose, he would kill Greffa with his hunter's spear. The Barradik would kill him in his turn, of course, but that did not matter. For Greffa would be dead and Shiva's spirit avenged.

21
Ogre Forest

The forest frightened her.

It was a world more strange than any other, a world of darkness, shadows and green filtered light. Although she had ventured here before (more often than she had admitted to any of her tribe), those trips had followed well-worn tracks that took her quickly to her destination. This time, running ahead of the Barradik, running ahead of the stampeding mammoth herd, she had plunged headlong among the trees without thought of finding a trail.

Her flight had saved her life. No Barradik would venture into these gloomy depths, and the mammoth had turned aside at the wall of trees. But now she was lost, disoriented and there were strange noises all about.

Shiva looked around her. Corridors of trees stretched out in all directions, rising from tangled undergrowth, gripped by twining creepers, proud giants that threw a summer canopy above the land, blocking out the sky.

There was life here, life in abundance. It leaped and skittered through the upper terraces, rustled in the undergrowth, lurked in bowers and dens. It called to her from the treetops, whispered to her all around. She could smell it, sense it, hear it, sometimes even see it, gray-brown shapes flitting on the very edges of perception, small creatures that lived short lives surrounded by abundance.

And by danger.

There was danger everywhere in the vast, cold, tribal lands. Danger from the hunting pride, the charging bull, the blinding storm, the raging torrent, the wailing spirit and the howling nightwing. But nowhere was there so much danger as in the forest. She thought of the wolf packs that roamed these shadows, fearing nothing. She thought of the boars, bristling beasts of such infinite bad temper that they would charge anything that moved and seek to rend it with their tusks. She thought of the bears, which shuffled through the undergrowth in search of berries, nuts and honey, towering hulks that did not hunt, yet so powerful they could crush a woman's skull with a single blow of one massive paw.

And even these were not the masters of the forest, not the most fearful creatures to be found here.

There were signs in the forest—markers left by her secret friends so that any member of the clan might find his way in places where he had not been before. Doban had taught her some of it, and now she frowned in concentration as she attempted to remember, fervently wishing she had paid him more attention. They were all natural signs, she recalled, so subtle not even a hunter of the Weakling Strangers would know them for what they were.

She searched her mind for Doban, and he rose up before her inner eye, squat and powerful, dark and strange, so vivid to her imagination that she could smell his familiar, musky scent. His hands reached out to break a twig, just so, in a certain way; and that was a sign. He curled the toes of one broad, flat, bare foot and crushed a leaf; and that was a sign. He loped away from her in that curious, shambling gait of his, grinned at her with enormous teeth, embraced a tree trunk, then scraped away a tiny patch of bark; and that was a sign.

She remembered now, part of it at least, but perhaps that part would be enough. It would have to be, she thought, for if she could not find her way to her secret friends, she would be as dead soon as the Barradik had wished her. She began to move forward with great caution, her eyes flickering everywhere, selecting her steps so that she made as little noise as possible. She moved slowly, partly from caution but as much from weakness. Her body ached from the beatings the Barradik had given her, and the muscles of her back and shoulders had stiffened so badly they were almost rigid. She felt hungry. She had eaten some roots and a few grubs since entering the forest, but they were little enough. What she needed was warmth and rest and proper food.

She wondered if she would ever find warmth and rest and proper food again.

She wondered too at her ordeal. Much of it puzzled her. She could understand why Weaver of the Barradik had seized her by the water hole. It must have seemed to her suspicious that she was there with the body of the Hag and apparently trying to hide it. But later, at the Barradik camp when she stood trial, the elders had scarcely listened to those who found her, had not listened at all to anything she herself might have had to say.

Instead, the fat chieftain Greffa had made an angry speech in which she denounced enemies and murderers and those who wished ill on the Barradik and spoke of the Shingu in terms so disparaging that Shiva's heart had leaped in anger despite the terror of her own position. Those Barradik who listened were inflamed by Greffa's words. They cheered themselves hoarse when, finally, Shiva was formally condemned to death.

Why were the Barradik so anxious to destroy her? Not the Barradik, she thought suddenly—Greffa! It was the Barradik chieftain who was so anxious to see her dead, the chieftain and some other members of the council. Not all the council by any means: just one or two of the purple-painted women; and of them, Greffa was most anxious. Why?

It was hard going in the forest. Away from the beaten tracks, the undergrowth was tangled and full of burrs and thorns. They had taken away her weapons, her axhead, her flint knifeblade and the bone club they claimed was stained by the Hag's blood. Now she carried a stout wooden staff, a branch found on the forest floor and stripped as best she could. It was little enough, but it was something, and she used it to slash a way through bushes and tangled clumps of vegetation.

Why did Greffa so desperately wish her dead? She had never before met the Barradik chief, let alone caused her any injury. She had known of Greffa by name and reputation, but that was all. And how could Greffa have known of Shiva, who was no more than an orphan of the Shingu tribe?

An orphan who found the Skull of Saber, a soft voice whispered in her mind.

Was that it? Was it because she had found the great cat's skull? She knew, as all the Shingu knew, the Skull of Saber might be chosen as Star Totem at the Jamboree.

And yet Shiva could not quite believe it. Killing her would make no difference at the Jamboree. What was found was found and could not be returned to oblivion. Even if Shiva were dead, the skull would still be carried to the Jamboree. Her death would not prevent its being chosen, if that were the will of the Mother.

Chosen by the Hag!

The thought had not occurred to her until that instant. It was the Hag who made the choice of totem at the Jamboree. And now the Hag was dead. Would that make a difference? Shiva did not know.

And new Hag or old, why should that make Greffa wish to kill—

She spotted a sign! Shiva stood stock-still, staring, scarcely able to believe her good luck. There, caught up in the branches of a bush, a fallen leaf was twisted in the hauntingly familiar way. It was a sign! She reached out to touch it, then drew back her hand. Let it be. It was a sign. Now she must search for more. With signs, she might find her way.

She turned her back on the leaf and moved, as she had been taught, in a widening spiral. This way, Doban had told her (and the lesson had been reinforced by Thag and Heft the Hunter), she was certain to pick up more signs, provided she paid close attention and the sign was not too old, for an old sign might become overgrown or otherwise obliterated.

Even in her excitement, Shiva did not lose track of her thoughts. As she moved cautiously outward from the leaf, her mind worried the same problem. Why did Greffa wish her dead?

Another leaf! She had found another twisted leaf; and beyond it a weathered scraping of bark, exactly as Doban had shown her. She stopped to sight herself between the two and saw at once two more leaves and a broken branch. Suddenly the way ahead was clear, the sign now obvious as a cavern painting by the Crone. Strange how it called to her once she had seen it. She had never really followed signs before, only played at learning it to please her secret friends. Now, suddenly, it was like a track, a trail. She began to move more quickly.

Why? Why did Greffa wish her dead? What did Greffa have to gain from the death of one lone Shingu orphan girl? Nothing. She gained nothing. There was nothing possible for her to gain.

Among all the sounds of the forest, there came a sound that was too close to her. Shiva stood very still and listened, sniffing the air for any trace of scent. There was nothing now, but the sound reminded her of something large, like a bear, moving through bushes. Was it a bear?

Still nothing, which was unlike a bear. The great creatures feared nothing and did not stalk, so blundered loudly through the undergrowth as they lumbered to whatever destination called them. Unless the bear had stopped for some reason.

Unless it was not a bear. Shiva felt her heart pounding. It sounded so loud in her chest, she feared it must attract danger to her, but she could do nothing to still its beat. She waited. If not a bear, what? The sound did not come again, which meant the creature was not moving, or had begun to move more quietly. Or that she had made a mistake about the sound. She did not think she had made a mistake.

She hoped it was a bear. Bears were not too dangerous as long as you did not approach them closely. Even if it moved again, she could probably climb a tree and hide until it lumbered past. Unless it saw her and became curious, she thought it would leave her alone. But what if it were not a bear? What if it were a wolf?

She did not think it was a wolf. The sound was wrong. Besides, the adults of the tribe assured her constantly that wolves did not like to attack humankind. Except that Shiva had once been hunted by a wolf, attacked by a wolf, nearly killed by a wolf, whatever the adults said. If the Mother had not sent Doban to save her, she would be dead by now. Doban had severed the wolf's spine with his teeth.

A chilling thought occurred to her. What if it were a boar? Of all the creatures of the forest, the boar was among the most dangerous. It was a beast that attacked without warning, respected nothing and moved fast. Any encounter with a boar was always trouble, usually more trouble than a girl alone could handle. Was it a boar? If it was a boar, she should definitely climb a tree and hide.

Yet there was still no repetition of the noise, which did not sound like a boar. Boars snuffled and routed and charged at once if they saw anything they particularly disliked. There was no stealth about them, just brute force and rage.

Cautiously Shiva moved on, still following the trail of signs. The sound did not repeat, and after long moments she began slowly to relax. All the same, she moved close to trees that were easy to climb.

What would Greffa gain from her death? What did Shiva have that Greffa wanted? Nothing.

The sign trail curved in a wide arc and she noticed the going had become easier. There was still no track, but the undergrowth was more sparse and in places actually looked as if it had been beaten back. She found herself moving faster now, despite her aching muscles.

Was there any reason why the chieftain of the Barradik should wish her dead? Try as she might, she could think of none.

Frowning, Shiva stepped into a clearing and knew at once she had been careless. The clearing was empty and there was no sound, yet she felt eyes upon her. She stopped, wondering if she should try to go back. But back where? She could make little speed through the undergrowth. Anything that stalked her here would have no trouble catching her.

Besides, the feeling might be wrong. There was no scent, no sound. The small sounds of the forest had stopped. Birds no longer sang or fluttered through the branches. A stillness hung about like winter fog. A master of the forest was nearby. Nothing else could cause such fear.

Wide-eyed, Shiva took a hesitant pace forward. She swung her head around, peering almost wildly into the trees. There was nothing, neither sight, nor sound, nor smell. Was there anything there? Was there really anything there?

Another step.

Should she call out? But what if it was a boar, or a bear? Sometimes a loud noise frightened predators away, but as often it enraged them, caused them to attack.

The sound came to her right and a little behind. She swung around as the creature broke from the undergrowth. It shuffled toward her, flexing its huge hands, a monster so ugly, so dangerous, so terrifying that its image haunted the worst nightmares of her race. This was the thing the tribe called ogre.

"Thag!" screamed Shiva in a shout of purest joy. And she ran to hurl herself into the creature's arms.

22

The Crone's Ordeal

It was a dry, still night, crisp with frost and filled with stars. The ringfires stretched like jewels across the plain, marking encampment after encampment. Distantly, there was the sound of drums and the click of sticks on bones. Closer, there was a low, approaching chant, escorted by flickering torches in a serpentine procession that meandered slow as melting ice in the direction of the Shingu camp.

Renka watched fearfully from her temporary shelter near the ringfire. She was able to stand and even walk now—slowly, limping—but still felt weak and had almost no resistance against cold, which set her thigh throbbing and her body shivering uncontrollably. But here, in the ringfire glow, leaning against a stout support post driven deep into the hard ground, she felt well enough. Besides, there was much afoot this night, and she was still chief.

She found her stomach clenching as the torchlit procession approached closer. Only the Crones dared walk abroad at night, and their murmured song of magical protection unnerved all who heard it, unnerved Renka more than all the rest, for the fate of her tribe was in the hands of the Crones that night. Nonetheless, she held her place and showed nothing. Close by, two women squatted, watching her, spears close to hand. Beyond them a party of five men, similarly armed. Their faces, caught in the dancing firelight, were hard and solemn. Few in the tribe knew all that had transpired, but all knew there was trouble in the air, and most guessed it grew in Barradik soil.

What, Renka wondered, would the next few moments bring. And hot on the heels of that thought came another: Would that I were strong again!

Strong enough, she told herself firmly. You are strong enough. You walk. You talk. What more is it that you wish? If you have to fight, you have failed, however strong you are. Besides, you will be even stronger in the morning.

She feared the morning. The celebrations would begin at dawn, although the tribes would have gathered an hour before then. There would be song and dance and prayers to the Mother. There would be contests and feasting. But when the great light of the sun disappeared in the west, the conclaves would begin.

What would the conclaves bring? Disagreement, for certain, bitterness and hate. Accusation and counteraccusation such as the tribes had not seen for generations. All that; but would it go beyond all that? Would chief set against chief, or worse, tribe set against tribe? Would there be death at the Jamboree? Would there be war at the Jamboree?

If there was death, it would, perhaps, be her death. In combat she could scarcely hold her own against a child, let alone Greffa of the Barradik or such of her cronies as might make a move. But that was no matter. What mattered was war, for war—against the Barradik—would raze the name of Shingu from the annals of the nations. However great their disaster had been, however punitive the mammoth stampede, the Barradik remained by far the most powerful of the tribes; and the Shingu remained among the weakest.

But before the morning, there was still this dreadful night.

Her gaze locked on the hypnotic motion of the torches, Renka wondered grimly at how this fearful

220

time had come about. First there had been the finding of the skull, a stroke of great good fortune for her tribe.

With the skull in Shingu hands, it was inevitable that it be offered as Star Totem. To have done otherwise would have been a selfishness beyond imagining, for did not the magic of the Star Totem benefit all the nations? Should the Shingu try to keep the magic of the skull for themselves alone? It was unthinkable. Thus the offering of the skull was good and, if accepted, would bring much good to all the tribes.

Where, then, had it all gone wrong? What actions or inactions had provoked the monstrous evil that stalked the land? The old Hag murdered, she whose task it was to select the Star Totem at the Jamboree. Shiva dead, she who had found the skull. Renka brought close to death, she who led the tribe that held the skull. And overhanging it all, the wrath of the Barradik nation, which was jealous of the Shingu and claimed Shiva of the Shingu had killed the Hag. Such ill fortune. More ill fortune than the tribe had ever known.

The chanting was closer now, softly seductive but with a warning lilt that threatened subtly, chillingly. Out there in the night, the river of torches stopped, the head of the procession so close that

221

she fancied she could see dark shapes beneath them. Despite her closeness to the ringfire, Renka shivered. Every shape a Crone. Every shape a witch of ruthless power. They had met, so it was known, to select a new Hag from among their number. But Renka knew they also met in judgment. For the Crone of the Barradik would accuse the Shingu Crone of plotting to procure the old Hag's death. And the Shingu Crone must answer. And her answer must be judged by all the Crones.

Who would be believed, the Shingu or the Barradik? Renka had sat in judgment on many a dispute, using common sense and observation to sift out the truth. But the Crones had their own ways, dark tests and sinister magics. And if the one accused stood guilty in the night, the bones would point so that she sickened. An empty shell would be returned to the chieftain of the Shingu. It would walk. It might even retain some words of simple speech, but it would not be the Crone. It would scarcely be human.

They were coming. Renka strained, but could make out little. Dark shapes were moving outward from the procession, shadows in the starlight flitting toward the Shingu camp. They resolved themselves into the figures of three women, one squat and hunchbacked, limping, one heavily tattooed and little older than Renka herself. And the third, the third was the slim, familiar figure of the Shingu Crone. She walked between her two companions, slowly. Did she shuffle? Had her soul fled from the pointing bones?

Her eyes—if she could only see her eyes! The eyes of those robbed of their souls were blank and lifeless, like the eyes of a corpse. If she could only see the eyes, she would know.

Two of the women stopped without a word. The hunchback threw back her head and howled a challenge to the night sky in chilling imitation of a wolf. Her tattooed companion answered with a wailing ululation that called up memories of the nightwing. The Shingu Crone stepped from the penumbra into the flickering firelight. Her head hung like one lost in meditation, or rendered mindless by the pointing bones.

Her eyes, Renka whispered, *let me see her eyes!*

There was no challenge from any Shingu guard, no move to help or escort the lone figure. The Crone was feared throughout the tribe. She walked by night, in darkness. She walked alone like a cat.

Her eyes, Renka prayed. *Dear Mother, let me see her eyes!*

The Crone straightened, turned toward her. Firelight fell across her wizened, granite face. Her black eyes glittered.

Renka stumbled forward, arms outstretched, a flood tide of relief welling in tears from her eyes. "Sister, you are safe!"

"We are none of us safe, Chief Renka," the Crone said coldly, extricating herself from the other's embrace. "Have you strength enough to talk with me?"

"Strength enough," Renka echoed, smiling, nodding. And indeed, she did feel better than she had throughout the night.

They walked in silence to the temporary longhouse, smaller built than was the custom, but with a well-stoked fire. By the time they reached it, Renka found she was breathing heavily and had to lie down on a heap of hay and skins piled near the blaze. But she waved away the Crone's offer to minister to her and instead asked urgently, "What has happened, Sister?"

"Mother," the Crone whispered softly.

For a moment Renka stared at her, uncomprehending. Then what the Crone was saying reached her. "Mother?" she echoed. "I should call you Mother?" Excitement pushed her upright into a precarious sitting position. "You are Hag?"

224

"I am Hag," the Crone confirmed.

Renka sat silent, staring at her ancient companion, her mind a jumble of unspoken questions, unexpressed emotions. Eventually she asked, "Were you challenged?"

"On the death of the old Hag?" The Crone nodded. "The Crone of the Barradik accused me."

"They did not believe her?"

"They did not believe her."

"What of the Barradik Crone?"

"She died." Just that, flatly.

Renka opened her mouth to ask, saw the Crone's expression and thought better of it.

"There was talk of poison," said the Crone. "Where Crones gather, there is always talk of poison."

"She had many enemies," Renka murmured. She could find no pity in her heart for the Barradik Crone or any Barradik. She was only sorry it was not Greffa and the entire Barradik council who were dead. She looked directly at the woman squatted by her side. "Does this end it?"

But the Crone shook her head. "No, this does not end it. This is merely a beginning."

"What will happen tomorrow?" Renka asked. She was still shaken by the news. There was none as qualified to become Hag, but somehow it still seemed impossible. "Will you select the skull as Star Totem?"

"I will," the Crone confirmed.

"They will say it is because you are Shingu."

"Of course they will say it is because I am Shingu. If I chose the purple gemstone, they would say it was because I once loved a Menerrum warrior. What they say does not matter. What they do is all that matters; and what they do depends on what they *can* do. We may safely ignore all nations save one, Renka. Only the Barradik have cause for action and the power to carry it through."

"So," asked Renka, "what will the Barradik do?"

"The Barradik will do what their elders tell them. They were always an obedient nation—too obedient for their own good. So let us not ask of the Barradik. Let us ask rather what the Barradik elders will do. Let us ask especially what the Barradik chieftain will do."

Renka watched her, waiting. The Hag was in her longhouse and the Hag was Shingu. Tomorrow the Skull of Saber would be chosen as Star Totem. What a future for the Shingu! What a future for the little tribe she had guided through these years— if the Shingu survived.

"The Crone of the Barradik was a weak woman," the Crone mused. "I always thought her too weak for a Crone. She permitted others of the tribe to dominate her. She challenged me only because Greffa ordered her to do so."

"How do you know?" asked Renka curiously.

"She told me." The Crone glanced at her with hooded eyes. "Before she died."

"And Greffa wished to challenge you because she thought you would choose the Skull of Saber as Star Totem?"

But the Crone was shaking her head. "Any Hag must choose the Skull of Saber. It is magic of a different order from the Giant's Thighbone: a choice so obvious it is no choice. If I did not make it, then another would. Only if the Barradik Crone became Hag would the Giant's Thighbone remain Star Totem, and the Barradik Crone had no chance of becoming Hag."

"Then why—?"

"Because she fears me. That much is obvious. And she fears me because she has something to hide. That too is obvious. A more difficult question is why she sought the death of Shiva. The girl was no threat to her." The Crone moved and stretched to ease cramped muscles. "But all this is specula-

227

tion, and we have no more time for speculation. We must plan, for the Jamboree begins tomorrow."

"What do you believe will happen, Sis—Mother?" Renka asked.

"I believe Greffa will move against us—move against the Shingu. Perhaps not openly, for stealth is more her way. She might wish to move against me, but she will not do so now that I am Hag—the dangers would be far too great. Thus, Renka, she will move against you."

"Against me?"

"You are chieftain of the Shingu. You must have suspected there would be danger for you in this matter."

Renka nodded dumbly. She had suspected. She had certainly suspected.

"It is my belief," said the Crone, "that you need fear no open challenge. Whatever motivates that Barradik, it motivates her to move secretly, by stealth. I believe your life may be in danger—at least for the duration of the Jamboree."

Renka looked at her without emotion. "What can I do to protect myself?"

"Naturally, I shall call on the ancestors to aid you, but that is not enough. The ancestors are notoriously disinterested in the world they left behind. It would be well if you were guarded."

"It is not seemly that a chief go to the Jamboree with guards," Renka said.

"Your guards will not appear to be guards. It is known you have been ill. Feign greater weakness than you feel and they will pass as nurses. Select strong, swift women for the duty—no less than five. And instruct that young hunter Hiram to join them. He is brave and skillful and hates the Barradik for what they did to Shiva." She stared thoughtfully into the fire. "I shall not easily forgive them that myself." She stood. "Let us sleep, Renka. Tomorrow is an important day."

23

Secret Friends

He ran ahead, into the clearing, rolling like one who walks on a raft, then reared up, stretching to his fullest height. "I am Thag!" he roared toward the cliff face. "I am Thag, your chieftain, strongest of the clan! Come out, come down and see what Thag has brought!"

A hideous face appeared to stare suspiciously from a cave mouth, then another and another. A hum of conversation rose like bees into the air. Then, almost simultaneously, two young clan males climbed down the sheer rock as easily as if it were a tree. At once, clansmen and -women poured from every cave mouth to swarm from the cliff like ants. They called excitedly to one another, and Thag, a male larger than any who appeared, encouraged them with shouted promises and ex-hortations.

"Quickly! Come out quickly. Thag has brought you something from the forest! Doban—come to me! Hana—where are you, Hana? You must come! Whatever you are doing, you must come!"

And they came readily enough, creatures like humankind, yet not like humankind, men and women both with hair that covered much of their bodies, beings with ridged foreheads, sloping brows, and massive jaws. They climbed with al-most unimaginable speed and skill, moved stooped on the ground with a crouching, threatening gait. They were quarrelsome and noisy, males and fe-males both, but the males more so than the females. Two rolled out from the crowd, locked together snapping, growling, gouging. Thag ignored them, as did all the others.

A tiny yellowish-white-haired female pushed her way to the foremost rank and stared impa-tiently at Thag. "Well," she asked sharply, "what foolishness have you found in the forest that makes you interrupt the work of the entire clan?"

But Thag showed no annoyance. He made sev-eral small, excited dancing steps, brushing aside a smallish male who had ventured too close. "See," he said. "See, Hana. See, see, see!" He gestured with one hairy hand.

In shadow, among the trees, Shiva saw the gesture and stepped out, smiling. There was an immediate uproar. The entire clan descended on her like the mammoth stampede. Instantly, she was surrounded. Hands reached out to touch her, tug her wolf skin, groom her hair. Arms embraced her. The warm scent of the clan was everywhere. She breathed deeply, joyously. She had been away too long. Now she was home.

"Back!" Shiva heard the voice from somewhere in the crowd. "Back, you idiots! Give the child room! You'll crush her! You'll suffocate her!" Hana pushed through and the males fell back hurriedly. Hana (shorter now than Shiva herself, Shiva noted with surprise) gripped her arms fondly and pressed a flat nose to hers in the clan kiss. "You . . . welcome . . . Shiva," she said haltingly in the language of the tribe, then repeated it in her own clan tongue for the benefit of those who listened: "You are welcome, Shiva. Our caves are your caves. May you stay a thousand years." Once these elaborate protestations had actually been necessary, for there had been some in the clan slow to accept the Weakling Stranger girl. But those days were gone. Although she still could not call all of them by name, she felt warmth and love from everyone.

A big male was standing shyly behind Hana, almost as broad and muscular, it seemed, as Thag himself. He was staring at Shiva intently with a curious expression on his face. He made a small move forward, then stopped. Something about the body posture jolted Shiva's memories. Her jaw dropped. "Doban . . . ?" she whispered.

The big male nodded.

"Doban!" Shiva screamed, and ran to him and hugged him. He slid one arm around her and looked around uncertainly. "Doban!" Shiva gasped. "You are so big! You have grown so big I hardly knew you!"

Doban nodded, pleased. "I am big, Shiva. Big and strong—almost the strongest of the clan!" He hesitated momentarily, then added, "After Thag, my father."

"You are strong," Shiva repeated, knowing how important strength was to the clan. "Today you could bite the head from a bear, not just a wolf." This last was in clan tongue, so the others could hear. Doban flushed with pride, for he was known to have killed the wolf whose skin Shiva wore, and killed it when he was no more than a boy. He had not actually bitten off its head as Shiva claimed, although he had certainly killed it with his teeth, so the exaggeration was small.

"You look as if you have been trying to bite the head off a bear," Hana put in, staring pointedly at Shiva's cuts and bruises. She turned on Thag. "You are a fool, Thag. Could you not see this girl needs rest and attention?"

"I brought her here," Thag muttered sullenly. He looked around angrily for someone to hit.

"I'm not—" Shiva began.

But Hana had already taken her gently by the arm and was leading her toward the nearest cave mouth. They entered the gloomy galleries and caverns that were the city of the clan. As they did so, Shiva realized suddenly how tired she felt. The aches and pains in her body had long since blended into a throbbing whole, which desperation had enabled her to ignore. Now the throb became a giant heartbeat that threatened to engulf her. She stumbled a little and was grateful for Hana's steadying arm.

"You see?" Hana murmured. "You need rest and red meat. You look like my Thag when he has been fighting. Except he is always fighting, even now when he should be making ready to step down and leave the clan to a younger man." She glanced

234

across at Shiva with concern in her brown eyes. "Someone has been beating you."

They climbed through passageways that left Shiva more exhausted with every step she took. Eventually, Hana led her into a dry cave high up in the cliff where gray light filtered through an opening half covered by a clinging bush. A burly form lay on a bed of twigs and dried grass, one outstretched leg wrapped in the broad leaves of a healing plant.

"Here is someone to keep you company," Hana said cheerfully.

The burly form turned. Brown eyes locked on hers. Teeth flashed in a slow, spreading smile. "Hello, Shiva."

It was Heft the Hunter, the same Heft who had once carried her through the forest depths for her first meeting with the clan. Shiva smiled at him in return. "You have hurt your leg, Heft," she said.

"Later for talking," Hana said severely. "Now you rest." She took Shiva to another bed against the wall, near the comforting embers of a small glowing fire. Shiva stretched out obediently, suddenly very glad she had no more need to run, no more need to hide, no more need to make decisions. "Sleep now," Hana ordered.

To Heft, Shiva said, "What happened to

your . . . ?" She sighed. And then it was too late, for warmth stole over her and carried her into sleep.

She awoke fully, as an animal awakens, without transition between sleep and wakefulness. Her entire body was stiff and sore, but for all that she felt much better. Heft was still in the chamber, but had moved from his bed and was seated by the entrance, looking out across the forest clearing. He must have sensed she was awake, for he turned.

"You slept long, Shiva."

She rolled from the bed and walked across to join him. It was morning now, and in the clearing below, those of the clan were moving about their daily tasks. She squatted beside Heft, feeling the high body heat he generated. "It is good to see you, Heft the Hunter. Are you well?"

He gestured sourly toward his leg. "Except for this."

"What happened?"

"A boar moved faster than I did. No matter. It has healed clean and is almost better." He looked away from her, as he always did when it was necessary to ask something of a personal nature. "You too have been injured . . ." He let it hang, letting his posture ask the question.

Shiva told him. She started with the discovery

236

of the body at the water hole and told him everything that had happened until the time Thag found her in the clearing. She told him of her pain and her fear and her bewilderment. Although he knew little of the tribes (all Weakling Strangers were one to him), she told him of the Barradik and of Greffa and the hill where she was taken for execution. She told him of the mammoths and of her own escape. And in the telling, she felt an enormous sensation of relief, as if the fear and the pain wrapped up inside her had begun to drain away.

When she had finished, Heft said, "You did not kill this little woman, this Hag."

Puzzled, Shiva said, "No. No, I told you. I only found her—her body. I never knew her before then. I never even saw her before."

"She was killed by a woman with a puckered face," Heft said. He sucked in his cheeks and pursed his lips in a caricature expression.

Shiva blinked. She had seen such a face before, at her trial in the Barradik encampment. It belonged to a Barradik elder who fawned on Greffa. Shiva searched her memory for the name. Saft. They had called her Saft! She stared at Heft the Hunter. "How do you know this?" she asked.

"I saw it done." Heft shrugged.

"You saw it? You saw the old woman killed?"

237

Heft grunted. "In the clans, we often hunt by night. It is good sport and good eating. The old woman often walked our hunting grounds at night—I cannot say why. But she did no harm, so we left her alone. Sometimes I watched her, for she did strange things with plants and bones. She could not hear or smell very well, so it was not difficult to watch her. The one with the scars struck her with a wooden club."

"And you saw it?"

Heft nodded. "I saw."

"What did you do?"

He shrugged. "Nothing. The Strangers' affairs are not my affairs. The old woman died. Not at once, but soon. The woman with the scars carried her to the water hole and left her there."

Saft of the Barradik had killed the Hag! Suddenly much started to come clear. If Greffa knew a Barradik had killed the Hag, it would explain why she was so anxious to condemn Shiva. With Shiva stoned to death, who would seek further for the murderer of the Hag?

A further thought occurred. Perhaps Greffa's motives were even more personal. Saft and Greffa were obviously very close. Was it possible Greffa might have *ordered* Saft to kill the Hag? If that was the case, she would certainly want to find someone else to blame as quickly as possible. What luck for her when Shiva was discovered on the scene.

Why would Greffa—or Saft herself—wish the Hag dead? Shiva did not know. But that meant little, since she knew almost nothing of the Barradik. Unless . . .

Unless it had something to do with the Star Totem. Little as she knew of the Barradik, she knew they owned the Giant's Thighbone, which had been Star Totem for as long as she had lived and longer. Everybody knew that. Perhaps Greffa, the Barradik chieftain, thought the Hag would choose the Skull of Saber in its place and so ordered she be killed. It seemed possible.

Excitement was growing in her by the moment. Whatever the reason for the murder, Heft the Hunter had seen the murderer. Once Heft told what he had seen, no one could ever again accuse Shiva of the crime.

"You are sure of what you saw, Heft?" Shiva asked.

"Oh, yes." His attention was taken by something going on in the clearing, so she tugged at his elbow. He looked around in surprise. "Yes, Shiva, I am sure."

"Would you recognize the scar-faced Stranger again if you saw her?" This was important. Those

239

of the clans often had difficulty recognizing the people of the tribes, who all looked alike to them.

But Heft nodded. "I am hunter," he said simply. It meant he had an eye for detail.

"Heft," Shiva said, "will you come and tell my people what you saw?"

Heft blinked at her. "Your people?"

"My tribe. And the people of another tribe, the Barradik. Will you come with me and tell them what you saw?"

"Come to your people?" asked Heft.

"Yes. Will you come, Heft? It is very important to me."

Heft said, "I will not come. The people of the tribes would kill me."

"No, Heft—no! They would never—" She stopped, staring at him as if she saw him for the first time. He was right. She had been so involved in her own concerns, it had not occurred to her to think what she was asking. Of course the people of the tribes would kill him—or try to. Just as they would try to kill any of the clans who ventured from their forest depths. However much Shiva loved them, the people of the clans were hated by the tribes. How could she have imagined her tribe or the Barradik would have listened quietly to the story of an ogre?

She sighed. "You are right, Heft. I did not think."

"He is right, but nonetheless he must tell what he saw."

Shiva swung around, startled. Hana had entered the cave, the looming figures of Thag and Doban behind her. "You heard?" Shiva asked.

Hana nodded. "Enough to know Heft must tell what he saw. Otherwise Shiva's people will continue to believe Shiva killed the woman who walked by night. This would bring dishonor to the clan, for is Shiva not as much of the clan as she is of the tribe?"

"But Heft says rightly that the Weak— that the people of the tribes will kill him," Thag ventured unwisely.

Hana turned to glare up at him. "Then you must protect Heft, mustn't you?" She reached out to poke her massive husband in the chest. "Are you no longer strong, Thag—the strongest in the clan?"

He growled then, deep in his throat, not at all displeased.

24

The Star Jamboree

There was silence, as total as the silence of the deep caves, all across the plain. In the gray light of the false dawn, the grassland took on a strange appearance, packed full of unmoving shadows.

The world was waiting.

It was a fine morning, chill, fresh, clear and dry, with no clouds in a lightening sky. A pink glow spread slowly, gradually illuminating the thousands of crouched figures on the plain. Nothing moved. There was a stillness that seemed almost infinite, a silence so profound it was almost tangible.

Then came the first sound—a high, clear, call of a single female voice that crooned a greeting to the rising sun.

The song wove a hypnotic spell, emphasizing

rather than destroying silence. Its plaintive notes called with strange authority toward the east, encouraging the great fire to awaken.

And awake she did. The first sight of the rising sun was greeted by a tiny murmur of appreciation from a thousand throats, a hum that rose like bees, then died away at once to silence.

The woman's song continued as the night turned slowly into day and the crouched shapes across the plain resolved themselves into a recognizable form.

Here, kneeling, facing east, were the swarthy Nagorma, the right hand of each woman whitened with chalk. Beyond them, kneeling, facing east, the Karunbara, every hunter wearing the elaborate horned headgear blessed by their Crone for ceremonial occasions. Beyond these, kneeling, facing east, spreading like a vast carpet of autumn leaves, the Barradik tribe, with its yellow-faced warriors and purple-painted elders. Beyond them, kneeling, facing east, the tall, thin figures of the Thorangando, men and women alternating, each with a single, speckled feather pushed into the hair.

So they spread, the tribes, across the plain, kneeling, facing eastward to the rising sun. Here the Shingu, a small tribe now greatly elevated since its Crone was chosen Hag. Here the Shama with their multicolored hair. Here the Labo, here the Rak,

243

here the wise Tomara, here the strange Lees, who were ruled by men, here the Hengenu and the Menerrum. Here, in this one spot, sweeping like the plains themselves, were representatives of every human nation in this vast, cold land.

The sun climbed further from her sleeping pit beyond the far horizon, and the single singing voice was joined by one other, so sweet and pure it might have been a child's, yet issued from the throat of an old Shama woman with the scarring of the forehead that marked her as a Crone. The voices interwove with one another, climbing, swooping and embracing in the chill stillness of the morning air.

Then came a third, a fourth, and then a man's voice, deep, melodious and strong. The song was one of joy for light and life, a hymn to the Mother, a remembrance of the dreamtime, a greeting to the Mother's sun.

And now, like rolling thunder, all joined in the singing, men and women both, tribe after tribe, until the entire plain was filled with song.

And the sun rose. And the Jamboree began.

Here men gathered to discover who among the tribes could throw stones the farthest. There a group of men and women both sought barter for furs. Here women sat in rows facing one another, chanting. There young men of every tribe preened and strutted through a storytelling contest, which was actually an exhibition designed to attract young women who might find them suitable as husbands. Here paints for sale. There talismans blessed by a distant Crone.

Hiram stared fitfully at the display, wondering how he could get close to Greffa. She seemed to be always accompanied by a whole contingent of armed men—no less than twelve at any time and often more. He had no fear at all of what these men would do to him when he killed her, for he was resigned to his own death and half looked forward to meeting Shiva once again in the dreamtime. But with such a guard, how could he get close enough to kill her? The Barradik were a powerful nation, its elders arrogant; and none more so than its chieftain, Greffa. None approached her without invitation, neither Barradik nor members of any other tribe. How then might he approach her?

But the problem, he thought, might solve itself. He and the women around him had been given the task of guarding Renka; and Renka, he knew, must meet with Greffa in the Great Conclave where the tribal totems would be unveiled for all to see and the Star Totem chosen. They met without guards, of course, or even weapons, protected by the witchcrafts of their respective Crones, but there was that moment when the leaders first came formally together, with their retinues, before the conclave actually began. At that moment there was a mingling, and in the mingling there, surely, would be his opportunity. All it required was a moment. He could use the hunter's trick of surprise and it would be done before anyone realized what was happening. Afterward would be of no matter, for Shiva, his love, would be avenged.

Soon, Shiva, soon, he thought. But for now, he must apply that other hunter's trick, of patience.

Without signal or instruction, a vast space, free of people, opened near the center of the plain. The jostling crowd around it suddenly fell silent, turned toward the space and waited, watching with intense expectation. For a long instant nothing happened, then, into the circle, crept a weird and frightening figure.

He was wrapped in furs so dark they might actually have been black. His face was daubed with mud, his nose striped and his eyes ringed white. He carried in one hand a short, barbed spear.

The figure explored, as an animal explores, sniffing the ground, skittering from one area to another. Then, his territory discovered, he leaped once into the air and darted toward the circle edge, bran-

246

dishing his spear. The crowd fell back with an audible gasp. The mud-daubed man threw back his head and laughed, then made another dart toward a different part of the circle.

"I am Hibley!" he called out. "I'll eat your ears for dinner!"

Hibley, thought Chief Renka, half her mind elsewhere, *the first demon of the dreamtime*.

Hibley began to dance, a sinuous, discordant movement, broken by unexpected leaps and darts. From somewhere near the edge of the crowd there came rhythmic clicks as drummers struck polished rib bones with short, thin sticks. The sound produced was sharp and dry, louder by far than might have been believed, and unforgettable. The rhythm caught Hibley and held him, so that he walked the entire perimeter three times around in exact accordance with the beat. At the end of his third circuit, he was joined by another mud-daubed demon.

Renka watched the action listlessly. She felt fearful and a little feverish, her thoughts brittle, tending to topple, clicking against one another like knucklebones in a game of chance. Around her ranged the women of her guard, and Hiram, his face strangely wild today, his eyes distracted. Although that, she supposed, was only to be expected. He had been very fond of Shiva, as they all had been, and carried a great burden of guilt about her death.

What would happen this day? A part of her raged at the Barradik for their treatment of Shiva, raged at Barradik arrogance. But the part was pushed down, hidden. For Renka, ill and weakened though she was, remained the tribal leader who must face the reality of every situation. And the reality here was the reality of power. The Barradik were numerous, were strong, were the inheritors of a warrior tradition. That was the reality of their power, a power the Shingu could not match.

Hibley and his cohorts had formed themselves into a straggling line that spiraled in upon itself, then, as the rhythm changed, was flung outward like a long, slow whiplash. The demons that comprised the line twitched and leaped and jumped at frequent intervals to show the increase in their power as their number spread within the dreamtime.

Across the ring from Renka, Greffa watched the dance with fascination and enjoyment. She had always loved to see the ancient stories of the dreamtime reenacted, and these demon dancers moved with great precision and skill.

Saft sidled up and squatted beside her in that

small open space reserved for tribal chiefs. "It will soon be time," she muttered.

Greffa nodded. "Yes."

"Our men are ready?"

Greffa said nothing but glanced about her casually. Saft followed the direction of her gaze. While all attention was on the dancing and other entertainments, Barradik warriors, split into groups of ten and twenty, had mixed themselves among the other tribes and now spread like a yellow patchwork throughout the entire gathering. It was an interesting deployment, for it meant that wherever disagreement might arise, the Barradik could move to stamp it out with ruthless speed. So much better, Greffa thought, than mass confrontation.

"Will you let the new Hag make her choice?" Saft whispered, her words distorted by the twisting of her mouth.

Despite herself, Greffa chilled. The Shingu Hag was the real danger, a greater danger than the whole remainder of the Shingu tribe. Had she not already poisoned the Barradik Crone? Very quietly, Greffa said, "No. I shall challenge her right when the totems are laid out. I shall not give her time to make her choice."

Excitedly, Saft asked, "What are you going to say, Greffa?"

Greffa shrugged, as if the matter were of small importance. "I shall say that she is Shingu, thus the Shingu totem should be withdrawn." She glanced at Saft and smiled. "In fairness, you understand."

Saft nodded, her scarred face contorted in a parody of an answering smile. "Yes, in fairness." The smile died. "But they will object."

"Of course they will object! Or try to. Why do you think I have our men where they are? You will find, Saft, there will not be too many objections, and those few that are voiced will come from the Shingu. My men have orders not to interfere at all with the Shingu."

Frowning, Saft asked, "Is that wise, Greffa?"

"Very wise," Greffa murmured. "Most wise. For when the Shingu object, I shall accuse one of their number of killing the old Hag precisely so that such an unfair situation should come about. I shall tell them how Weaver and her men found the brat Shiva with the old Hag's body at the water hole. I shall tell them how she was tried under Barradik law and found guilty. Who will listen to Shingu objections then?"

Two serpentine processions were approaching through the crowd, interweaving with one another, then sweeping in a single wave toward Hibley and his straggling, leaping, twitching line. The dancers of these processions were painted in broad stripes of red and white, symbolic of the Mother and her helpers.

There were screams from the mud-daubed dancers as they ran with stylized steps in frantic attempts to escape those representatives of the Mother who pursued them. But the pursuit was relentless and the demons were soon caught.

There was communal dancing then and song, to celebrate the demon rout. Then great fires were lit and meat roasted and the feast began, each tribe contributing a share of food.

And after the feast more singing, and after the songs wrestling, more stone-throwing and spear-throwing contests to decide which warriors and hunters were most skilled. Greffa watched the wrestling with consuming interest. She was pleased to note the Barradik men did well. They were strong and heavy and well fed, so only the muscular men of the Lees gave them any real competition. She was even more pleased to note how well her warriors were placed now, mixed in with every portion of every crowd. There would be a general gathering for the selection of the Star Totem, which was by far the most important aspect of the Jamboree, and when it came, her men could move with the crowds and take up their final positions without attracting any attention at all.

A perfect plan, she thought, perfectly conceived and soon to be perfectly executed. Greffa glanced away from the wrestlers, a smug half smile playing around her lips, and found the glittering black eyes of the Shingu Crone, now Hag, upon her. The smile died abruptly and she turned away. When she glanced back moments later, the Crone had disappeared.

The light began to fail, and with the growing twilight came an air of expectation. Ringfires were lit, not alone around the camps, but dotted widely across the great plain. There was a gradual exodus toward the natural amphitheater where tribal representatives were already gathering.

Soon, very soon, the Star Totem would be chosen.

25

The Dead Walk

It is time, the Crone thought. She was crouched in a cave within one of the rocky outcrops that rose from the floor of the great hollow. She wrapped the ceremonial bearskin around her shoulders and slipped from the cave mouth like a shade, keeping well clear of the nearest pool of firelight. She stood in shadow for a moment, watching. The totems were already laid out on the great natural table of stone a little to one side of the center of the giant hollow. She could see almost all the tribal offerings from this vantage point: tortured wood turned to stone, the bones of beasts, a polished jewel taken from the stomach of a mammoth, the Giant's Thighbone of the Barradik and, off to one side yet dominating them all, the Skull of Saber Shiva found. She could still hear the gasp that had gone up when it was first revealed.

Greffa plans something, the Crone thought. *She will not let me select the Skull of Saber without a fight.* She felt a burning hatred of Greffa then, of the entire Barradik nation. Shiva had been precious to the Shingu, and the Barradik had killed her. It might have been the mammoth herd that had trampled her, but it was the Barradik who had killed her just the same.

She pushed the thought aside. It was enough to worry when Greffa made her move. In the meantime, she could hear the sounds of the chieftains and their retinues begin to gather.

It is time, thought Hiram. He moved casually away from Renka, slipped unobtrusively from his place among her guard. He moved into shadow and remained in shadow. He had not far to go: Greffa and her retinue were close. The flint blade he carried was small, a weapon that would scarcely be noticed in the crowd, but in a hunter's hand it would be enough—one slash and Greffa's throat would open. No one recovered from such a wound.

For you, Shiva! Hiram thought.

The amphitheater was enormous, made, so the storytellers said, when a huge stone fell from the dreamtime to bury itself in the earth. Its vast natural terraces and rocky outcrops swallowed even this great congregation of the tribes, so he could see only groups and clumps, marked by firelight and torchlight. The rest were lost in gloom, hidden in shadows, wandering the empty spaces beneath the solstice stars. No matter—he knew where Greffa was; and that was all he needed to know.

He moved forward to mingle with the retinue around her. In his hand, the flint blade was slick with sweat. *For you, Shiva*, he thought again. Then he was seized from behind.

Hiram struggled like a wild thing, but the two Barradik warriors held him firmly. The Barradik around them made way with little curiosity as he was dragged into the shadow of a rocky overhang.

"What do you think you're up to, Shingu?" one warrior hissed threateningly into his ear.

"We've had our eye on you, Shingu," the other told him almost cheerfully. "All day, we've had our eye on you."

Hiram drove his elbow into the nearest stomach and had the satisfaction of a grunt of pain before a fist smashed into his mouth in retaliation. He tasted blood.

"You've been creeping around after our chief," whispered the one who had struck him.

"We think you mean to do her an injury," snarled the other, a little breathlessly.

"And we don't want that to happen," said the first, striking him again with such force that Hiram's fingers opened nervelessly and the stone blade clattered to the ground.

"Look," said the one Hiram had hit, "he had a knife."

"Naughty boy." The other grinned, his face pressed close to Hiram's own. "But we've got spears. Shall we stick you with our spears? Chief Greffa would be pleased if we got rid of some dirty little Shingu who wanted to do her an injury. So shall we stick you with our spears?"

From behind them, in the depths of shadow, came a low, spine-chilling growl.

It is time, thought Renka. She looked around for Hiram, but he was no longer among her retinue. Renka frowned. It was unlike the boy to shirk his duty. But there was nothing she could do about it now. The chieftains were gathering in preparation for the ceremony, and it was time she joined them.

She gestured to her guards, who fell back obediently, and began slowly to walk alone down the hill. As she neared the gathering place beside one of the bonfires, the tall form of the Lees Chief emerged from the darkness to walk beside her. The others seemed to be already in place, waiting.

She glanced up at the Lees Chief, a handsome, well-muscled man with a hunter's walk, and wondered, not for the first time, at a tribe that actually allowed its men to lead. He nodded to her and smiled.

It is time, thought the Crone again, and stepped from shadow into the pool of firelight. The sounds from the terraces ceased at once.

She turned slowly, full circle, her eyes watchful. Bonfires burned on the terraces as they did on the amphitheater floor, and she could see groups of white faces picked out by the firelight. They stared back at her, excited, expectant and a little fearful. Strangely, she could see no single group of Barradik and wondered where the major portion of the tribe congregated.

She turned back toward the low, broad rock table where the totems were spread out and was struck at once by an intuition of danger. It shivered along her spine like a serpent and struck her brain with such force that she almost staggered. She looked around again. The danger was out there, on the terraces, or beyond.

But as quickly as the intuition came, it faded.

The Crone shook her head. What danger could there be? What danger that she had not already recognized? Sometimes her intuitions were proved wrong when she was under too much strain. She forced herself to relax and walked with grave dignity toward the center.

"Hag!" whispered a lone voice in the darkness.

"Hag!" said another and another. And on the instant, the chant was taken up across the terraces until it swelled from the great amphitheater. "Hag! Hag! Hag! Hag! Hag!"

Then she reached the center and the chiefs moved out to greet her. The attendant Crones swept in like spiders from their selected crannies, and the entire gathering fell slowly silent.

She saw Renka, eyes still bright with fever but steady enough. Renka had courage, one of the greatest leaders the Shingu ever had, although neither Renka nor the tribe really knew it. No matter, she knew it. As Crone she had known it and as Hag she now knew it. She would support Renka for as long as she wished to lead.

The Shama chief stepped forward, raised both arms above her head, and asked in a loud voice, "Crones, do you avow your Hag?"

"*Hag!*" screamed the Crones in unison and danced around her, pointing. She remained stock-still, her eyes moving from Renka to Greffa. Greffa, she thought, scarcely deserved to lead. It was all power and prestige to her. She cared little for the welfare of her tribe, excepting where the welfare of the tribe impinged upon the welfare of its leader.

The dance ended and the Crones spun off into the darkness, leaving her alone again. The Menerrum chief stepped forward. "Hag," she asked, "will you now select the next Star Totem?"

"I shall so do—" she began in the ritual response. Then she stopped as Greffa interrupted.

"My friends," said Greffa easily, "it seems to me the choice cannot be made."

The Crone watched her, waiting, black eyes glittering in the firelight.

Something came out of the darkness like an attacking bear and suddenly Hiram's arms were free.

Impressions jumbled. He saw the two Barradik warriors flung together as if they were the playthings of a child. He saw them slide to the ground.

The scent of evil was strong in this shadow place beneath the overhanging rock. Red eyes stared at him. Hands reached for him.

Hiram ran. Stumbling, in the grip of an old terror, Hiram ran.

———

"So you see . . ." Greffa was saying, her hands spread, as if in innocence and helplessness, a reasoned appeal from one who had made her case.

Frowning, the Shama chieftain said, "The Star Totem has always been selected by the Hag." She had always disliked Greffa.

"Indeed it has," Greffa agreed, "but until now, the Hag herself has been selected fairly."

The Crone spoke for the first time. "Do you suggest, Barradik chieftain, that I was not selected fairly?" Her tone was soft, even mild, but her eyes glittered more fiercely than before.

A growing murmur was sweeping through the watching throng. Only those on the low terraces could hear, but the word was being passed along. Soon all would know there was a confrontation.

Greffa avoided looking at her directly. "I mean no disrespect to the Crones of our nations," she said loudly. "I do not question the right of the Crones to select a Hag. I only say this: The Hag before us is a Shingu, and the Hag before her was murdered by a Shingu!"

So it was to be the same accusation, thought the Crone. Shiva dead was as useful to the Barradik as Shiva living—more useful, for Shiva dead could not defend herself. But that did not mean Shiva would go undefended. There, if nowhere else, Greffa was mistaken.

"Who is this Shingu who murdered my predecessor?" the Crone asked with hissing menace.

But Greffa would not be intimidated. "The girl Shiva!" she said loudly. "The very girl who found that abomination of a skull!" She swept her arm around in a dramatic gesture.

The Crone stepped forward, mouth already opening, when she was stopped short by a clear, familiar voice.

"I have killed no one!"

The dead walked. Shiva stepped into the firelight.

"Shiva . . ." the Crone whispered.

Greffa stared at the slim figure without speaking for a moment, then recovered. "Seize her!" she shouted. "This is the girl who killed the Hag!" Her voice reverberated across the terraces.

Another voice, the voice of Saft, echoed, "Seize her! Seize the murderess!"

And from the terraces, the cry was taken up. "Seize her! Seize the murderess!"

So that was it! The Crone's eyes swept around, to confirm what her keen ears had already told her. Greffa's tribesmen were scattered throughout the congregation of tribes. They were starting the calls to seize Shiva—and the calls were being taken up!

"Seize her!" screamed Saft again. She emerged from behind the group of tribal chiefs, flanked by a twenty-strong party of Barradik warriors.

It had all come to this moment, the Crone thought. She glanced across at Renka, who was waiting for her signal. A nod, a single, small inclination of the head, and Renka would order the Shingu hunters to Shiva's aid.

And blood would spill.

The Crone's eyes locked on Renka's own. Her head remained motionless. If Shiva was seized, it would be Barradik justice, a rerun of her trial with Greffa as accuser and the Barradik nation as judge. If the Shingu acted quickly, Shiva might escape, but blood would spill.

Saft's men swept toward Shiva. And still the Crone made no sign.

"Killer!" Saft yelled. She ran. She closed on Shiva. Slowed. Stopped, horrified. And screamed.

Something broad and terrible loomed from the darkness behind Shiva. Eyes shone red in the firelight. Arms reached for Saft, embraced her. The creature's face pressed closer to her own and the monster spoke in human tongue. "You killed the old woman, Scar-faced One," it said. "I saw you

262

kill her with your club!" Then all Saft could feel was the increasing pressure of the arms around her; and all she could hear was her own voice screaming.

"*Ogre!*" shouted someone in the crowd.

The warriors with Saft had frozen. Now they ran forward to her aid. But then the ogre who embraced her was joined by another monster, then another. They poured from the darkness, a nightmare horde, each one more dreadful than the last.

"My men—to me!" Greffa shouted. But her men were distant, scattered on the terraces.

The ogre stream became a torrent. They flanked Shiva two—four—seven deep, then spread outward like a growing stain across the floor of the vast natural arena. Panic screaming began in the terraces.

The Crone remained motionless, face blank, watching. Two ogres seized Greffa, who froze at their touch, a look of horror on her face. More of the creatures flooded in. Not fifty or a hundred, but a thousand ogres easily—and still more came. The Crone's eyes flickered to the terraces and she saw squat shapes there as well, swarming from their rocky clefts, emerging into firelit pools from darkness. And then she heard it:

"*Save me, Hag!*"

The scream had come from Greffa, now surrounded by the monsters.

The Crone glanced across at Shiva and held up one hand. Shiva nodded slightly and the movement of the ogres stopped. There was still screaming from the terraces, but the Crone ignored it. "Who killed the old Hag?" she asked softly.

"She did!" Greffa shouted in her panic. "She did—Shiva!"

"Who killed the old Hag?" asked the Crone again.

"Shiva—she killed—"

"Who killed the old Hag?"

"Saft!" yelled Greffa. "She did it! She was the one!"

"On your order, Greffa! On your order!" Held between two ogres, Saft's face contorted with fear and rage.

"Who killed the old Hag?" asked the Crone relentlessly.

"Saft killed her on my order!" Greffa shrieked. "Oh, get them away from me! Get these things *away* from me!"

"I am Hag," the Crone said softly. "I have no power to command ogres." She turned her back and walked away.

26
At the Water Hole

They sat on the same rock from which Shiva had seen the body in the water hole, their legs hanging over into space. There were no cats there today, but a fox had crept out to drink.

"I hate ogres," Hiram said, shivering, the sound of his words startling the fox into flight.

"They are my friends," Shiva said.

"I know," Hiram said, "but I can't help it. They frighten me."

"They came to make sure my own people did not hurt me," Shiva said. "The whole clan came—and the clans beyond the clan. Thag told them to, of course, but they would have come anyway."

"Yes," Hiram said. He sat lost in thought for a moment, then remarked, "They frightened Greffa, too."

"Thag and Heft both wanted to kill Greffa and Saft. They could not understand it when I asked them not to."

"I'm not sure I understand that myself," Hiram told her. "After what they did to you."

"Greffa's tribe would have sought vengeance," Shiva said. "Once begun, the killing never stops."

They sat together, side by side on the rock overhang, lost in their own thoughts. The Skull of Saber was chosen as Star Totem. Saft was exiled from the Barradik and Greffa was no longer chief. So many changes in so short a time.

"Shiva . . . ?" Hiram said uncertainly.

"Yes, Hiram?"

"Will you ah . . . will you ah . . . will you ah?" His head began to bob up and down uncontrollably, like that of a bird.

Shiva looked across at him in astonishment. "Will I what?"

Hiram flushed. "Will you ah . . . will you ah . . . will . . . ?" He looked at her expression. "You won't, will you?"

"Not now," Shiva said. "I'm far too young." She jumped up and raced down the rock.

After a moment, Hiram rose and followed her.

Epilogue

There's a lot of guesswork about prehistory. One of the most interesting guesses is that women were the leaders. This runs contrary to the old idea that men led the tribes because they were bigger and stronger and made sure everybody was well fed by going out to hunt.

It's true the men did go out to hunt, but that may not have been as important as it sounds. Studies of today's primitive communities—peoples living much as our Ice Age ancestors did—show that hunting accounts for only one fifth of the nourishment consumed by the tribe. The remaining four fifths comes from gathering and scavenging, digging up roots and finding fat grubs under leaves. Gathering and scavenging has always been women's work.

267

There are other pointers as well. In 1908 a carved limestone statuette was discovered on the north bank of the Danube at Willendorf in Austria. It was a female figure that archaeologists thought might be a representation of a goddess.

But this Venus of Willendorf, as the figurine came to be called, was only one of many. Similar Venus figures have been discovered all over Europe—and in prodigious quantities. After a while it dawned on archaeologists that they were not dealing with a whole slew of different goddesses at all. Ice Age people, it seemed, were actually making different images of only one. They thought the supreme deity was female.

And if god is a woman, then it's unlikely that the leader of your tribe will be a man.

Shiva's tribe was led by a woman, as were the disgraceful Barradik and almost all the other tribes. But more importantly, their spiritual advisers (their shamans, as we would call them today) were women too—old, wise women, the Crones of the tribes, who knew the powers of herbs and the hidden ways of nature.

I also believe that the Crones were connected with the cave paintings.

In 1879, a nobleman named Don Marcelino de Sautuola entered a cavern at Altamira in Spain, raised his torch and found to his astonishment that he was standing in a veritable gallery of prehistoric art so sophisticated in its execution, so technically advanced in style, that experts of his day promptly accused him of painting it himself.

But other, similarly painted caverns were soon discovered, and opinions had to be revised. To date about 230 caves containing prehistoric art are known. The great majority are in France and Spain, but additional examples have been found in Italy, Portugal and the USSR.

Some of the paintings are done in outline only. Others are filled in with a flat wash, or shaded in colors. Drawings made by dipping the fingers in wet clay or paint can be seen. Hand imprints are also featured. These seem to have been made by applying a paint-daubed hand against the wall, or placing a clean hand flat then spraying around it a mouthful of pigment, usually a solution of white clay. The colors used were ground from natural deposits of mineral ore and mixed with animal fat, vegetable juices, water or blood, then applied with a stick chewed at one end to turn it into a brush. Animals were the favorite subject matter. But many symbols—lines, spirals, zigzag abstractions—and some masked human figures have also been found.

There are two mysteries connected with all of

this. One is what those symbols represented. The other is why the people of the Ice Age bothered to paint caves in the first place.

Today, of course, art is used to decorate our homes and, more formally, as displays designed to elevate the human spirit. This can't have been the case in prehistory. Painted caverns like those at Altamira give no indication of having been lived in. Even the notion of a primitive art gallery doesn't hold up. While sculpted cave art is generally found in shallow rock shelters or near cavern entrances, most paintings are deep inside.

At Niaux in France, for example, the first paintings are about 600 yards (550 meters) from the entrance. From cave mouth to the great fish at La Pileta cave, Spain, is even farther—about 1,300 yards (1,190 meters). A major feature of another cavern is so inaccessible that it requires you to risk life and limb swinging out from a natural window with one foot on a tall rock spur before it can be seen at all. So they weren't meant for general viewing.

But they weren't casual creations either. Enormous effort went into their composition. The Cro-Magnon artists often—indeed usually—worked in cramped, difficult conditions. Some paintings are so high that ladders or scaffolding had to be used.

The paints were applied in gloom and semidarkness, by the flickering of torchlight or animal-fat lamps. Smoke smudges can still be seen on the walls.

The paintings themselves were intricate. They might be carved in high or low relief, modeled in clay or engraved deeply or finely and then hatched. The animals depicted—mammoths, bison, horses, deer, cattle, goats, and wild boars; with woolly rhinoceros, antelopes, cave lions, wolves, cave bears, birds and fish more rarely shown—were executed with a skill and grace that suggests a substantial investment of time.

Where did the artists find the time to produce such masterpieces? As you will have gathered from Shiva's story, life was hard in a world very different from our own. The whole of Scandinavia lay beneath a single ice sheet, like much of today's Arctic. Almost all of northern Europe was devoid of woodland, chill wastes of tundra broken only in the most sheltered spots by a straggle of pinewood.

Yet although survival in the Ice Age was difficult and all-consuming, Cro-Magnon people found something so important in art that they took time to paint the insides of several hundred caves. No one knows why, but I think the answer was magic.

Many anthropologists agree. Belief in sympathetic magic is widespread in primitive communities today, so it seems reasonable to assume it was equally widespread in prehistory. The theory of sympathetic magic is that if a representation of a thing is created, then the representation can be used to influence the thing itself. The notorious voodoo doll of Haiti is an example of sympathetic magic.

On this basis, the theory is put forward that the paintings were created to influence the success of the hunt. Although few human figures are portrayed, many of the animals are shown transfixed by arrows or spears. The fact that old artworks were painted over would support it too: Fresh magic would have to be made if not for each hunt, at least for each hunting season.

But it can't all have been about hunting magic. The reindeer is known to have been an important food source, for example, yet it is very seldom pictured. If the paintings were just magical aids to hunting, one would expect reindeer to have been the most prominently featured animal of all. Then there is the fact that some of the representations are composites. At Pindal, in northern Spain, for example, there is a painting of a trout with the tail of a tuna. Not even the most enthusiastic magician

272

will bother to cast a spell on a creature that does not exist.

Then too there is the art that does not show animals at all. In the Americas rock paintings are found that are similarly symbolic, schematic, or naturalistic. The intricate, mazelike Chibcha drawings from Colombia reflect the elaborate whorls and spirals carved into the world's most ancient monument at Newgrange in Ireland. The geometric zigzags and mythic (spirit) elements found in the Ice Age caverns of Europe show a striking similarity to elements in the rock art tradition of the Australian Aborigine.

There can be only a limited number of explanations for similarities of this sort. One, obviously, is migration, carrying a particular tradition of abstract art from one place to another as humanity spreads itself into new territories. But the migratory theory will not do. The similarities appear in cultures that have been isolated from one another for hundreds of thousands of years.

If we rule out migration, the next most likely explanation must be common experience. So what was the common experience that prompted Ice Age artists to paint symbols and spirits into their more naturalistic scenes? Some ingenious anthropologists have concluded that the ancient artists were moved to paint what they saw not in their normal waking state, but in trance . . . and I think those anthropologists are absolutely right.

If you look at shamanistic practice anywhere on earth today, you'll find it's 99 percent about trance. The witch doctor's eyes roll up, his body trembles like a leaf in the wind and suddenly he's gone, disappeared somewhere into the depths of his own mind to talk with spirits or cast oracles or walk with his gods.

The Crone in our story could do that as well, of course. She used secret plants and magic methods to liberate her spirit so it could take on the shape of a bird. And when she went into the depths of her forbidden cavern, she painted pictures of her adventures in the spirit world.

These visits to the spirit world, these trance experiences as we would now call them, were the secret of the Crone's magic, because primitive people everywhere believe absolutely that what is done in the spirit world can (and does) influence physical reality. Thus the paintings themselves would have become magic, because they depicted magical events.

But to the people of the Ice Age magic was a tool, something that helped them survive an environment so harsh we can scarcely imagine it. And tools are not much use if they remain buried in the dark depths of a cave. Thus portable magic was developed, engraved or painted on stone, bone, or ivory. In eastern Europe, as at the Czechoslovakian site of Dolni Vestonice, figurines were modeled in clay, placed in the ashes near a fire, and hardened by heat. Although wood may also have been used, no examples have survived.

This portable magic art includes figurines, necklaces, and bracelets, as well as decorated tools such as spear throwers and harpoons. The engravings seen on these objects often closely resemble those on the cave walls. So the Crone made her deep-cavern magic, and Shiva's people took it with them in their special decorations.

Which leaves only one question: Was this "magic" all imagination, or did some of it actually work? Could the Crone *really* send her spirit soaring to influence events at a distance in the body of a crow? Could her sister Crones really have left her mindless by pointing at her with a bone? Could all—or at least most of—the strangenesses in our story actually have taken place?

I think the answer might be yes.

—*J.H. Brennan*

Be sure not to miss the third book in J. H. Brennan's Ice Age trilogy, recently published by HarperCollins Publishers:

SHIVA'S CHALLENGE

"Release her hands."

Someone stepped forward and removed the twisted strips of bearskin. Shiva might have run then, but she did not. She was held by the power of the Crone's gaze, which was as strong as any bonds. Besides, where was there to run? Caught in the northlands in winter, she would be dead if she left the tribe.

The Crone's glance flickered downward to the skull bowls. Her voice was soft as the dry rustle of dead leaves. "Six bowls," she said. "All but one contain poison. Thus five are deadly; one is harmless." She looked back into Shiva's eyes and blinked once, slowly, like a reptile. "Drink!"

It was the Ordeal by Poison! The victim took one bowl and drank. If the Mother Goddess aided her, she chose the right bowl and survived. If not, she drank the poison and died a hideously agonizing death. Shiva had heard talk of the Ordeal before, but not like this. Always she had been told it was convened only to try one convicted of murder by the Elder Council, and even then only rarely. Did they think her a murderess?

"Lady Witch—" Shiva began, heart thumping.

But the Crone cut her off. "Drink!" she whispered again, with such fierce authority that Shiva's hand reached out toward the bowls.

With a massive effort Shiva stopped herself, controlled the fear in her veins, the pounding of her heart. She met the Crone's gaze with every ounce of courage she possessed. "Why?" she whispered, so quietly that only the Crone could hear her. "Why is this being done to me?"

Impassively, the Crone stared back at her. "It is your destiny," she said.

Shiva felt her hand move again, driven by an irresistible compulsion. *Which bowl?* All looked alike. Their contents, dark, fluid, thick and viscous in the firelight, looked alike and smelled alike. *Which bowl?* From only one might she drink safely and survive. Five were filled with death. *Which bowl?*

There were no sounds at all around her now. Even the night creatures seemed to have stilled their cries, as if they were congregated in the outer darkness, watching. What had she done?

Slowly, so slowly, her hands crept forward. *Which bowl was safe?* And then a strange thing happened. The figure of her mother rose up in Shiva's mind. It was strange, for Shiva had never known her mother, who had died giving her life. But in her childhood years, Shiva had made pictures in her head, and those pictures, often as not, were of a handsome woman she called "Mother." Often she imagined that this handsome woman talked with her as mothers talk to daughters. Often, in her loneliness, she imagined this woman spoke of love.

Not that one! whispered the figure of her mother in her mind.

Shiva's hands moved away from the cup she might have chosen, moved toward another.

Not that one! the voice of her mother whispered again. *Take the cup at the end. Only that cup.*

Could she trust the voice? Her life depended on it. She reached out and touched the bowl at the end. She heard a gasp from the surrounding crowd, but the Crone's features betrayed nothing.

"Drink!" the Crone ordered.

She had made her choice. One bowl was as good as any other. A curious calm poured over her, and Shiva took the bowl and drank. The draft was oily and intensely bitter. It burned her throat and churned her stomach, leaving a foul aftertaste. She set down the bowl.

For an eternity there was silence and stillness. Then, without warning, her breath caught in her throat. She reached forward to steady herself on the table, but her arm would not respond. She felt her knees buckle, heard a ringing in her ears.

There was a sudden eruption of excited chatter among the watching women as she teetered. Breath rasping, limbs convulsing, Shiva pitched forward into darkness.